IS THERE ANY
TIME LEFT FOR GOD?

Kelley
THE WALK WITH GOD
MAY SEEM LONG BUT
YOU ARE NEVER ALONE

LOVE YOU
AUNTIE
JEWEL
8/25/13

IS THERE ANY TIME LEFT FOR GOD?

JEWELLYN GREER

TATE PUBLISHING
AND ENTERPRISES, LLC

Published by Tate Publishing & Enterprises, LLC
127 E. Trade Center Terrace | Mustang, Oklahoma 73064 USA
1.888.361.9473 | www.tatepublishing.com

Tate Publishing is committed to excellence in the publishing industry. The company reflects the philosophy established by the founders, based on Psalm 68:11,
"The Lord gave the word and great was the company of those who published it."

Book design copyright © 2013 by Tate Publishing, LLC. All rights reserved.
Cover design by Jan Sunday Quilaquil
Interior design by Jomar Ouano

Published in the United States of America

ISBN: 978-1-62510-303-1
1. Fiction / Christian / General
2. Religion / Christian Life / General
13.06.19

ACKNOWLEDGMENTS

Thanks be to God for this great gift of writing that he has given to me. God is using me in supernatural ways. I am able to bring comfort to people of faith and people of no faith through my writing, through my Facebook page interactions, and through my "ministry of being there."

Every day in my ministry God leads me. I could be in the subway, on the streets, in the grocery store, in the restrooms at work, on the internet, or at the beach, and God will use me to be a blessing to someone in need. I am so very thankful for the gift of listening, as many times, people just need me to listen, and when I listen attentively, I hear what they did not say, and when I open my mouth to pray, God directs my speaking.

I want to acknowledge everyone, anyone who I have been able to reach, especially through my ministry of being there and on my Facebook page. There are many who are being encouraged daily, many who were not afraid or ashamed to share their troubles with me and ask for prayer. Many of our prayers have been answered, and for those prayers that we have not yet received an answer for, we are still prayerful, knowing that God answers every prayer. We just need to wait patiently and to listen to his still, small voice.

There is no prayer too insignificant for God to hear, there is no need that he cannot supply, there is no problem that he cannot fix, and there is no crooked path that he cannot make straight. We just have to learn to walk in God's will, and no matter what happens in our lives as we walk with him, to give him the glory, because God knows what is best for us. We just have to trust him every step of the way and especially when we cannot see what lies ahead. God knows our needs before we ask. When he blesses us, we must remember to give him thanks and praise.

I want to encourage you to keep the faith, encourage those around you, and be a friend, not only to those you know, but especially to those you don't know, for as the Scripture reminds us, if we do it to the least of them, we are doing it to God.

May your walk with God be strengthened, and may you trust God to help you overcome all and any obstacles that you may face. Never be too quick to dismiss those you don't know or who are different from you, because you may be dismissing the most vital part of your puzzle. God brings people into our lives for a reason—just trust him.

Everything happens for a reason and according to God's plan. Your situation may be the solution that you have been praying about. Learn to look beyond your present circumstances and praise God in the midst of your struggles, and the way before will become clearer as God reveals his marvelous wonders in your life. Learn to spend quality time with God in prayer, because a friendship with God brings peace, joy, and love. God makes time for you, but do you have any time left for God? Is there any time left for God in your busy schedule?

CHAPTER 1

Marion opened her eyes slowly, stretched, and said, "Thank God it's Friday. TGIF."

Marion began to mentally go through her entire weekend from what to wear to work, keeping in mind happy hour after work with her girlfriends to her Sunday evening book club meeting. As she slowly surveyed the room, her eyes rested on her husband's sleeping frame on the sofa. Harold had been sleeping on the sofa on and off for years when he did not do what Marion wanted him to do or when he let his anger get the best of him, and it did not phase Marion one bit.

Marion gave a passing glance at Harold who was just rolling out of the sofa bed, and said to herself, *If you ever want to get out of the dog house and into my bed, you know what to do*, and without giving Harold a second thought, Marion walked to the bathroom to brush her teeth.

As she was coming back from the bathroom, Marion's cell phone rang. At the same time, Marion saw Harold jump up and heard when he mumbled something, but she just ignored him and grabbed the phone from the dresser. It was her friend Chloe. "What's up, girlfriend? Happy Friday!" she said.

As she greeted her friend, Chloe, Harold echoed loudly, "Happy Friday! That is what I mean, Happy

Friday to your girlfriend and not even so much as a good morning to me. I've become a door mat in my own house."

"Right back at you, girlfriend," Chloe responded.

"So, what's shaking?" Marion asked, still ignoring Harold's ranting.

"You should know," Chloe said. "You always have it hanging out, Marion, but I was just checking to confirm our after work happy hour session today."

"It's definitely on," Marion said.

"So, what are you planning on wearing today?" Chloe asked.

"At the moment, nothing but my toothbrush," and annoying you know who can't touch this, Marion said, teasingly, and she demonstrated with her hands for her husband's benefit.

Sure enough, Harold heard her, and he looked at Marion and said loudly, "Go on, I'm sure your friends already know that you are not sleeping with me and are laughing at me."

Chloe overheard what Harold said, and she responded by asking Marion playfully, "You got the man on the sofa again? What did he do this time?"

"Girl, don't spoil a good day asking me about Harold." Marion then hooked the phone between her neck and shoulder and still ignoring Harold, walked to her overflowing walk-in closet. She said, "Girl, I really need to straighten this closet out, it's a mess, but not right now. At the moment, I need to find something appropriate for work and play. I need to dress interchangeably, as who knows where the night will end.

"You go girl, but you and I both know that is not your problem, finding something to wear." Chloe said. "Girl, if I was your size, the inside of a store would not see me, for we both know that you have a whole clothing department store up in there, and I won't ever need a layaway plan. My credit's always good with you."

"One day, you are going to reach your credit limit with me," Marion said. "I keep telling you that you should either get a real job or a sugar daddy like mine."

"Well," Chloe said, "I don't know about that, because for one, I could never hold down a real job, and two, a sugar daddy like yours I don't need, because, your sugar daddy sweetens your tea with one hand and makes you bitter coffee with the other. No offense, but if I had to choose, I would choose a man like our friend Tammy's husband, except that he is a Christian, and it will never work. We are too different. But you know, Eric is always so nice and respectful, and he shows Tammy so much affection.

"Sometimes it even seems rude, but I know he means no harm. They always seem to have it all together, not that I am comparing you both, which is like night and day, but they always seem so calm, and they are always so tight and happy, so into each other. While you, on the other hand, are always fighting with your man, even though he gives you the best things money can buy."

"Girl, all that glitters is not gold, and I don't need to hear this right now," Marion said, "not when Harold and I practically hate each other."

"So," Chloe said, "why don't you try to make it better? After all, he affords you a good life. Me, I am struggling every day. I am glad that I have you and Tammy to sponge off of."

"Life is not always what it seems," Marion said, "but just make sure if you change your mind, Chloe, that you get a sugar daddy that could pay the bills and someone else who can give you the thrills."

"You are not right, Marion. You need Jesus."

"Oh my goodness, that could not be Chloe, sinner from hell and master of the fire talking!"

"It sure is, girl. I am just mimicking Tammy. You know, one day we should really take Tammy up on her offer and go to church, but I would feel so out of place as I've never been to a church in my life…

"Well, and I sure don't intend to begin now, so don't even go there," Marion interjected. "That is a conversation for another day, not today."

"Okay, okay, Chloe said. "Don't chew me out. I was just thinking that it would be nice to accept Tammy's invitation. If not go to church with her, we could at least attend one of her church functions. To be honest, I am curious as to why she is always ranting about her church of promise. We could at least attend a function at her church."

"And why should we, Chloe?" Marion asked.

"Well," Chloe said, "because she has never refused any of our invitations to go anywhere we ask, unless she deems it inappropriate"

"Well, it's her right to refuse and so is ours," Marion said. And as for inappropriate, it's not appropriate for her to be forcing us to go where we don't clearly want to go, like to her church.

"Come on, Marion. You know that is not true, and it's not like she is trying to convert us or something."

"And you don't think that is her ultimate goal, Chloe?"

"Well, I don't know about you, but I think it would be hard for anyone to convert an atheist, because it's the life we live and we defend it. I have never found myself having to defend my beliefs to Tammy, and she does not push her beliefs on us. She just holds on to her belief and her faith in her God and prays for us, as she says."

"Well, let her do that," Marion said. "I don't really want to have this conversation right now or anytime else for that matter, and for the life of me, you are the last person I expected to hear this from. Where is this all coming from, Chloe? Are you having second thoughts about your beliefs?"

"Oh no!" Chloe said. "But I don't think we are being true friends to Tammy in this regard, and even if it does not seem to bother her—"

"All righty then," Marion said angrily cutting her off in mid-sentence. "Leave it alone. If she is happy, we are. Call me later," Marion said, and she hung up abruptly.

———•◆•———

As Chloe hung up the phone, she sighed. *Poor Marion is so stressed out. I know she could not be so upset about our conversation. I think she is just using this as an excuse to take out her frustrations about Harold. I sense that something is not right with Marion, but I can't put my finger on what it is. The next time I talk to Tammy, I will ask her if she notices anything differently with Marion or if it's just me reading too much into what she usually says or from what I read between the lines. I am really worried about my friend.*

CHAPTER 2

As soon as Marion turned around, there was Harold blocking the door, and before Marion could click off the phone, Harold laid into her with one of his usual tirades that had kept him on the sofa, because when he was in this mood, Marion refused to share the bed with him.

"Marion!" he shouted, as if Marion was not in the same room.

Marion did not answer, as she knew what was coming and just let Harold continue ranting while she carefully selected her outfit for the entire day, from underwear to jewelry.

"Marion!" Harold shouted again.

"What, Harold? What do you want? If you are going to start this mess again, I am not going down that road with you, not today," said Marion.

"Mess! Mess! Mess! That's what our relationship has become, Marion, a pure mess. You don't sleep with me anymore—"

"It hurts, doesn't it?" Marion lashed back.

"You know it does," Harold said. "You don't cook for me or spend any time with me like you used to. You don't do anything for me, Marion, not one thing. All you care about is those tired, going-nowhere girlfriends you have, and God knows what you all do when you go out or who you do it with." I don't know why you treat me this way Marion, I really don't know.

"Well, let me tell you why, Harold, since you are obviously ignorant. My tired, going-nowhere girlfriends have come to mean more to me than you do. And you want to know why? They don't abuse me. They don't make me feel like nobody. They don't disrespect me. They allow me to be me, and you demand things of me as if I am the hired help, and you know what else Harold? What I do when I go out has nothing to do with you. You hear me? Nothing! I don't question where you go, who you go out with, or what you do when you do, and I really don't care."

"Then why are you still here, Marion. Why?"

"I could tell you why... No," said Marion, "you'll just muddle this up. Let me break it down for you, Harold. It's your money that pays the mortgage, my car note, the utility bills, my mother's nursing home, and it's your money that affords me the lifestyle I deserve after the way you have treated me all these years. You just can't stand it now that the tables have turned. I have taken a stand for myself, and I am controlling my own destiny."

Harold angrily shouted back at her, "Controlling your own destiny? You mean you would be *des tiny* without me," and he raised his thumb and index finger to demonstrate just how tiny. "I picked you up when you had nothing and made you something. I introduced you to this lifestyle that you now claim is all yours. Without me, Marion, you would have been nothing. You would be nothing! You hear me? And that meddlesome mother of yours would be living under a boat."

"Now, back it up there, Harold," Marion said. "You are an ungrateful dog. You forgot how my mother slaved for you? My mother loved the dirt you walked on until you started treating me like the same dirt you walked on. You deserve to pay for her nursing home, because it's the way you treated me that caused her breakdown. I just hope she lives to two hundred years and lets you pay for keeping her in the home.

"Let me tell you this, Harold, you had better check yourself, because when you married me, I was somebody, but you robbed me of my self-esteem, but it would be a cold day in hell before I allow you to rob me of my self-respect. Your money may have afforded me this lifestyle, but you sure did not give me this life. God did. He gave me this life that you so want to take away."

"Oh yeah?" Harold said. "Did I just hear you mention God? God who? Which God? Not the same God you are so offended by when Tammy talks to you about him? You know how to conveniently pull him out of the closet when you need him. It's a shame, Marion, what you have become. You don't go to church. I never hear you pray. I never hear you say, 'Thank you, God,' for your new car, for the clothes that you wear, for the food on your table, and for the roof over your head."

"And you do, Harold?" Marion asked. "Oh, I'm sure you do. You are doing it right now. You always believe that all the money that you have makes you all powerful, that you are always right. Well, guess what, ole moneybags? You are not all that. You should be thankful that this *nobody* spent your money to become a *somebody*." Marion pushed pass him to get dressed.

"Marion!" Harold shouted. "All I ever wanted from the day we met was for us to live a good life, have a family, go to church—"

"Don't even go there, Harold. You knew I was never a church woman. You wanted a trophy wife, and you got one. Your money is your family, your church, and your God, you talk about to me. Why don't you give thanks to your God for all that you have?"

"I used to, Marion, but I don't anymore because of my situation. My faith is not where it should be."

"And you blame me, Harold?"

"Yes, I blame you, Marion. I have made a few mistakes in our marriage, and you want to punish me for the rest of my life, but I am not going to take this anymore. I am not going to take it anymore. I am sick and tired of being just that, sick and tired. You don't sleep with me anymore. I wonder who you are sleeping with."

"Obviously not you, and I never will. I need someone who could fulfill my needs, and you fall short, Harold, real short in that department."

"I fall short?"

"Yes, Harold, you fall short. As a matter of fact, you just don't cut it that way for me anymore, not that you ever did."

"So that is the real reason for me sleeping on the sofa while you enjoy my sleep number bed? Well, it's not going to happen anymore. It's just not going to happen, Marion."

"Well, what do you plan, Harold? What do you plan to do?"

"You'll soon find out," he said, and he stormed out of the bedroom and went into the bathroom.

Marion's shoulders slumped; she sighed and shook her head, then said to herself, "Why do I put up with this?" *It starts like this every day before I leave the house, and it is wearing me down, but I will not let Harold and his foolishness not let me have fun today. It's TGIF. Thank God it's Friday. That being said, Marion pulled her shoulders up and threw her hands in the air and shouted, I have a full weekend planned, and nothing is going to hold me back. I have money in my purse and gas in my car, and I can't wait to jet on out of here, away from this miserable crap of a man.*

I have too much to do today, to be bothered with Harold. Luckily, this is not my weekend to visit Mom. She usually sees right through all of my hurts, and I hate to worry her with my problems, but it is comforting to know that she is always there, even to listen, but I could never tell her all that Harold has been putting me through, even though I think sometimes she has sensed it. Maybe I should go and visit with her, I always feel better after our visits but I have so much to do. Mentally, Marion began to go over all the tasks she had to fit into one weekend.

- *a dental appointment*
- *get fitted for my girlfriend's wedding*
- *Meet up with Chloe and Tammy after work today*
- *Tomorrow, I have my hair and nail appointment*
- *book club meeting*

- *I have to run by the mall and pick something up to wear to Margie's birthday party*
- *I need to pick up my laundry from the cleaners*
- *Oh, and I almost forgot, I promised my aunt that I would drop off some groceries for her, and I always save the best for last:*
- *my weekly massage with my Italian therapist who has hands to die for. That is one appointment I certainly will not miss.*

I started these sessions with my therapist to relieve the stresses in my life, but most recently, I have kept my appointments, not only because they were helping me physically, but it felt good mentally to just have a place of refuge from all of my worries if only for a few hours. It would have been nice if Harold was a different husband.

If only he was capable of giving me a massage. But, he is useless, and I wouldn't want his filthy hands touching me anyway. The only thing he knows how to do well is to be abusive, and I have too to do much this weekend to allow Harold and his negativity to disrupt my plans, because before you know it, it will be Sunday. Usually, by the time Sunday rolls around, I am so exhausted that all I want to do is to sleep half the day then get up in time to go to my book club meeting. I really don't know how I fit this all in, but trust me, if it means keeping up appearances, I'm in, not to mention any time away from Harold is a treat. Now why I am spoiling this beautiful day giving that loser Harold any more thought than I need to? He surely does not fit into any of my plans, and he never will. I am so tired of hearing him complain *about me not spending any time with him. And should I? I do make time to spend his money, and he should be grateful for that.*

As if on cue, Harold broke into her thoughts, and she heard him shout, "Marion! Marion, are you still here, or are you getting all dolled up to go and spend my money?"

"There he goes again," Marion said sadly. *He is now ready for round two, but I will ignore him. Tell me, which other woman would put up with his nagging, possessive, abusive ways as long as I have? His money is the only positive thing about him, and by him being the positive, I am fully charged to spend it. I have more clothes than I could wear. I have more than enough jewelry that one woman should have to tide me over should things change and I have to pawn them, and thanks to Harold, I have some solid investments that could take two children safely through college. But, for now, I am the only child I have to cater to, and my whims are endless. I could never have enough Coach, Prada, Jimmy Choo, or any of the other good stuff that Harold introduced me too. Well, yes, Harold may have spoiled me in the beginning, but it was a means to his end, and now, the end has caught up with him, and it's not at all what he imagined. Too bad! His end is my beginning. Now, it's all about me.*

If only all these things could make me happy. Marion sighed. My friend Chloe thinks I am so happy because I have so much, but *I have not been really happy in a long time.*

Sometimes I silently despise my friend Tammy for the life she shares with her handsome husband, Eric. They always seem so happy, so together. Wait a minute. Am I repeating

Chloe's words or what? But, fair to say, they seem very happy together. Tammy is always so upbeat and so positive. I never hear her complain. Instead she prays about everything. I wonder if this prayer thing really works. I'll admit I am curious sometimes, but I can't ever let her know this. I find myself using her phrases even though I have no idea what they really mean, but they do make a lot of sense. The other day I was feeling real low after a fight with Harold, and I found myself talking out loud, hoping someone would hear and answer me, and Tammy's words kept echoing in my ears, "Marion, neither me nor Chloe is the answer to your problems. Jesus is." But I don't know if this Jesus, God—whoever this person is that Tammy so believes in—is a real someone who could help me, but I really need help out of this situation.

Days like this, I feel like I am losing my mind. I just have these constant rantings amongst myself. It's a wonder I don't hear someone talking back to me. I wish I could tell someone what I am going through, the pain that I am feeling. But, you know what? I have become very good at hiding what I am feeling, but at what cost? To my friends, I seem to have it all, but on the inside, I am dying. I am so unhappy. Days like this, Tammy's words are forefront in my mind, "Prayer changes everything. Make time for God, and he'll make time for you."

I don't know about Tammy. She says the first thing she does each day is to give God thanks and praise then fit everything else into and around her schedule. Maybe she has something to thank her God for every day, but me, when I awake, I see Harold, and when he starts cussing, how could I ever begin a day in prayer or be happy, when all I want to do is to kill him? Maybe I should take Tammy up on her *offer and go to church. I am so tired of her asking me the same tired, old question. Is there is any time left for God in my busy schedule? God does not need my time. He made time. I am the one who needs him to make time for me when I am in trouble or distressed or sick or like right now. If he is as real as Tammy professes, I need him to extend to me his calming presence before I hurt Harold. I have been feeling this temptation more often than before. It would be so easy to cop a self-defense plea should I really yield to the temptation. But would I be able to live with myself after that?*

"Oh no! Now I am answering myself," Marion said. As she continued her thoughts, Marion surprised herself by saying out loud, "Lord, my thoughts are not right. I am here thinking about how to get rid of my husband. I really should try to pray to you as Tammy suggests. But I don't know you or how to pray. I have never prayed for anything in my life, because I've never believed it's something that actually works. How does one begin to pray, and me? God, you would never answer my prayer, you don't even know me, and I don't believe in you or go to church like Tammy." *I wonder how she finds the time. One of these days I will probably ask Tammy to teach me how to pray. Wait up, girlfriend, get your mind right. Today is Friday. People like you don't pray on Friday. They play on a Friday, so on that note, I am out of here.*

CHAPTER 3

Tammy was awakened by her husband, Eric, who stroked her eyes and kissed her with light, feathery kisses, and she smiled, rolled over, and hugged him tightly, and said, "I thank God for you every day, for the love and respect you show me."

"I know," Eric said. "I pray the same way. So could I thank you now in my own special way?"

"Not now, Eric, you know we have to give God thanks for this beautiful day and for all the many blessings that he has bestowed on us and for what he will do for us this day.

They both knelt then beside the bed and offered prayers of thanksgiving to God.

Eric and Tammy made it a habit to begin and end each day with prayer, not only for themselves, but for others, and today they were especially remembering their friends Marion, and Harold, who had been going through so much.

Tammy began praying. "Lord, we pray that one day Marion and Harold will just turn to you for the answers that they are so desperately searching for but in all the wrong places, and for them to just spend some quality time with you in prayer to allow you to work your purpose out for their lives. Lord, I don't know what else to do or say to help them, because every time I especially ask my friend Marion the same question, I get the same answer—that she does not have any time in her busy schedule for you. I know, dear Lord, that you could work her purpose out on your own, but she needs to accept you as the Lord and master of her life and watch you work, but until then I will just have to be the friend she needs when she needs me, until she comes to fully realize that there is not a friend like you—a friend who will be always there, who will never talk bad about her or judge her, and who will accept her just the way she is. Amen."

After they were finished with praying, Tammy and Eric walked hand in hand to the kitchen.

"Hon," Tammy asked, "do you want coffee or tea?"

"How about adding another choice?" Eric said playfully.

"Like what, Eric?"

"Well, coffee, tea, or me?"

"But, you know my answer already," Eric said, and started coming toward Tammy.

"Don't start, Eric. We'll never make it work this morning."

"And, so what?" Eric asked. "We both own our companies."

"Yes," Tammy said, "but we have responsibilities."

"Well," he said teasingly, "your responsibility starts at home in the mornings with me. You seem to have conveniently forgotten your Bible readings."

"What Bible readings?" Tammy asked suspiciously.

"Colossians 3:18 and 1 Peter 3:1. 'Wives, be submissive to your husbands as is fitting in the Lord.' He was all the while kissing her neck, lips, and eyelids.

"I have not forgotten, but I also remember his word in Ecclesiastes 3, that there is a time for everything and a season for every activity under the sun, and now is the time to get ready for work. We don't want to be late for work, and we need to set good examples."

"I am trying to set one here."

"Errric! We don't have time."

"Yes, we do, five minutes, Tammy. Five minutes!"

"What!" Tammy said. "I did not marry a five-minute man."

"Well then," Eric said. "How about ten minutes?"

He continued to kiss Tammy so passionately and looked at her with puppy dog eyes only for her. Tammy was unable to resist him and gave in to the demands of her wonderful, adorable husband and allowed him to take her back to bed, where they forgot about work and the rest of the world.

When they got up again, they showered together, and having set the tone for a beautiful day, they left for work. Marion backed out of the two-car garage in her shiny silver E-Class Mercedes, and Eric backed out in his BMW 6 Series Coupé while blowing Tammy a kiss, which she returned. And so the day began for Tammy and Eric—Tammy to her consulting firm and Eric to his architectural firm.

Tammy's business focused on real estate but also represented major construction firms in tendering bids for projects, as well as placement of personnel. Eric's architectural firm was well known for the design of major infrastructure in and around town. They both were successful, and life was even better now since Eric and Tammy became one through marriage. They were hoping that one day they would be able to link both companies together and leave a legacy for their children, if that was part of God's plan for them, but so far Tammy was not able to conceive, but they both believed that their best was yet to come and would continue to wait on the Lord.

CHAPTER 4

On his drive to work, Eric thought of Tammy, as he did after every time they were intimate. He would hope that she would get pregnant, but month after month he was so disappointed when Tammy did not get pregnant. *I guess God is preparing us for this dream that we have in our hearts and which we have no doubt that he will bring to pass in his own time.*

But, Tammy, despite her many disappointments, was the one who kept reminding me that God will give us the desire of our hearts in his own time and when he knows we are ready for a child, but I have to exercise much faith when she reminds me of this, because my desire to be a father, for us to be parents is so strong, even more so for me than Tammy I believe, that we will continue to pray and to wait, knowing that all things will work together for good to those who love God, and we sure do love the Lord. But each time someone announced at church that they were expecting, I couldn't help but wonder if it was because my love for God was not as strong as I believed. I wondered why Tammy was not getting pregnant or if God knows that a child will bring us much heartache like that boy Patrick for Sister Mary.

Sister Mary was a God-fearing woman who had seen her share of trials and tribulations. Her only son, Patrick, was breaking her heart, even more so than when her husband left her for a younger woman when Patrick was twelve. Up until that age, Patrick was a model child, but when his father left, he became rebellious and told his mother that he was never going back to church, because God did not love him or he would not have allowed his father to leave him for another woman.

No matter how much Sister Mary tried to explain to Patrick that his father's leaving was not his fault, he continued to blame himself and started hanging out with the wrong crowd. He went from daily fights at school to truancy to shoplifting and then to juvenile hall at sixteen.

When Patrick was released from juvie, Sister Mary said he was so different, and it seemed like he had graduated from the school of "hard knocks." He was no longer the same son Sister Mary knew and loved. He started stealing from her in sophisticated ways to support his drug habit, which later landed him in jail. It was during his incarceration that Patrick again found the Lord, and Sister Mary, who never gave up on him, was so happy. Patrick was set to be released in six months time, and Sister Mary constantly asked us to keep him in our prayers—that God would truly change him back to the wonderful creature that he created him to be.

So, maybe, just maybe God is trying to shield us from this kind of pain, so I will continue to pray and ask for God's guidance and direction. And right there in his car, Eric began to pray:

"Lord, who knows your mind? Your thoughts are not our thoughts, nor your ways our ways. We tend to get doubtful when we cannot see what lies ahead, but I will not become doubtful because you know just what I need, and I am confident that my faith is the substance of the things I hope for and the evidence of the things I cannot see. Lord, I know that you are the giver of all good things. I know that they who trust in you will not lack anything good, and like Scripture reminds us in Revelation 7, one day, we will hunger and thirst no more. The heat of the day will not strike us, and God will wipe away every tear from our eyes. So whenever I am tempted to question why we have been waiting so long for a child, I will refocus my thoughts on the other blessings in my life and pray for those who have children who have gone astray—parents who are at the end of their ropes trying to pull them back from the brink of despair—that God will change their unruly minds and instead give them hearts to serve him in mighty ways. All this I ask in the powerful name of Jesus. Amen."

Eric then made his usual stop at the florist and ordered flowers for Tammy. He had been doing this from the time he first met her and said he had no intention of stopping, as Tammy he said adored flowers.

I know they make her smile, and anything to please my beautiful wife, is all right with me. Eric said. *It's amazing just watching the way she fusses over the floral arrangements. She puts sugar in the vase with water, claiming the flowers will last longer, especially the roses, and she carefully removes all of the dead leaves or petals. Tammy's friends and clients are always sending her flowers, and if I was not secure in my marriage, I would be worried about her accepting them, but I know my marriage is rock solid. I keep it that way by keeping our marriage real, by doing nice things for Tammy, and she really, truly appreciates the little things I do for her.*

Eric recounted that one day Tammy forgot her favorite coffee mug at home, and he went home and got it for her, and how she had kissed and hugged him as if he had just given her a million dollars. *That's my Tammy*, he thought. *She is the love of my life, and I am continually thanking God for her, and the love we shared. I would plan special date nights for us. I would take her car and drop her off at the hair dresser on a Saturday morning then pick her up in time for a late lunch, but not before I had her car detailed. I don't understand it when I hear stories of other married couples having so many problems. I guess we are doing something right. But I honestly believe it's because of the love that we keep alive in our marriage, the respect we give each other, being there for each other, and most importantly that we pray together, putting God front and center of everything in our lives.*

Eric met Tammy at a ground-breaking ceremony for a new development project back in 1990. He said they were attracted to each other immediately and exchanged phone numbers. Eric admitted that it took a while for him to call her, as he was waiting to see if Tammy would call him first. So, they played the waiting game for about a month. All this time, Eric said he just could not get Tammy off of his mind, so he caved in and called her, and after speaking on the phone for almost half an hour, he had worked up enough courage to invite Tammy out to lunch, and she accepted.

From that first date, it seemed like Eric and Tammy could not find enough reasons to be together. They found they had so much in common, so much to talk about, that they really enjoyed spending time together. During one of their many conversations, Eric told Tammy that he grew up in a Christian family, but after college and working, he found more excuses why he could not make it to church or even to pray. Eric said he then asked Tammy if she was a regular at church, and she told him that she was and explained that she had a situation in her life that forced her to give her life to Christ when she was just fifteen years old, and had been a member of Church of Promise ever since. Eric wanted to ask the inevitable question, but it felt out of place. He wanted to know if she was a virgin.

He was blown away to learn that someone as beautiful and as smart as Tammy had been living such an exemplary life. This made her even more attractive to him as a woman, so much more desirable, and he began to wonder if he was deserving of such a woman. It was during this conversation that Tammy initiated the invitation to church, and Eric accepted.

After that first visit to the Church of Promise, Eric realized that it was the same denomination that he was raised in, and he felt right at home, and so going to church together soon became the norm. This raised questions and eyebrows, but Eric and Tammy maintained that they were just friends, and that's what they were, but they were becoming closer by the week.

One Sunday during the altar call, Eric recalled that the minister spoke directly to his heart. The minister asked one simple question that really got to him: "Is there any time left for God in your busy life?"

This question made him really ponder how he was spending his time. The question really hit home when the minister compounded the question by asking, "What if God were to put everything and everyone else before you. What if when you needed him he said, 'I don't have any time'? God always gives the best to us, so why should you give him what is left over of your time, talents, and resources and not the very best?"

Eric had thought that this was just too much food for thought, and as he began to ponder these things in his heart, the pastor extended an altar call invitation, and the choir started to sing.

> Have you any room for Jesus, he who bore your load of sin?
>
> As he knocks and asks permission, sinner, will you let him in?
>
> Room for pleasure, room for business, but for Christ the crucified,
>
> Not a place that he can enter, in the heart for which he died.
>
> Have you any time for Jesus, as in grace he calls again?
>
> Oh today is time accepted, tomorrow you may call in vain.

Room and time now give to Jesus, soon will
pass God's day of grace,

Soon thy heart will be cold and silent, and thy
Savior's pleading cease.

This is surreal, Eric had thought to himself. *I felt like
I was in a world of my own.*

Then he heard a voice, so quietly, so tenderly, so
gently say, "Son, I have been waiting for this moment.
If you just make a little room for me in your heart, I will
enter in."

Eric knew it had to be the voice of God, and he responded
by accepting the altar-call invitation. He dedicated his life
totally to God that day, and he later became a member of
the Church of Promise, where he pledged his time, talents,
and resources to the service of the Lord.

Six months later, Tammy and Eric were married.

*It seems like our being together was orchestrated from
above, and Tammy assured me that it was God's doing
and that we were evenly yoked, and the rest, as they say, is
history. I made a pact back then that I was not going to allow
anything or anyone to come before my God, and that I would
put all of my decisions and all of my choices before him and
that I would give him the very best of my time, talents, and
resources. It has become so much easier to fit everything else
and everything I do around the time I dedicate to God since I
am walking in the light of the Lord.*

At Tammy's urging, Eric became a member of the
Men's Fellowship and Bible Study groups. He volunteered

to be a life coach to the Little Wanderers Club. He was available as much as possible to the service of the Lord, and it always amazed him, because when he was doing things differently, he could never find time for anything else but his pleasures and business, but now that he was in service for the Lord, he could not be happier.

All that is missing from my life, our marriage, is a child. We have been praying about this, and I know in God's own time that he will bring it to pass. I know that Tammy will make such a wonderful mother, and she said that she knows I will make a wonderful father, as she watches the way I mentor the kids in the Little Wanderers Club. Tammy and I have a wonderful life together, and with God's help it will only get better.

Since I gave my life to Christ and married Tammy, life got sweeter. We are in a good place spiritually, mentally, physically, and financially. We have our struggles, but we have learned to take everything to God in prayer, and when we do, he takes our yoke upon himself and relieves us from all of the turmoil we face. Oh, how good it is to know I know the Lord, and as the song came to mind, Eric started to sing:

Through it all, through it all, I've learned to trust in Jesus, I've learned to trust in God.

I thank God for the mountains and I thank him for the valleys, and the storms he brought me through, and if I ever had a problem I know he'll solve it too. So, through it all, through it all, I've learned to trust in Jesus, I've learned to trust in God and to depend upon his word.

CHAPTER 5

Marion called Tammy as she was on her way to work.

"Tammy," she said, "I am so upset with Harold this morning. He is so tiring. He is driving me to drink."

"Well, Good morning to you to, Marion!"

"Girl, I'm sorry. I hope your day is going better than mine."

"It sure is," Tammy said, "and yours would too if you learn to begin and end each day with prayer. Now, calm down and tell me why you are not enjoying the start of this brand new day that the Lord has given us."

"Oh, no thank you, Tammy. I am not going down that Holy Ghost road with you this morning. I need to vent, and if you are not going to be the friend I need today, then I should call Chloe. She always seems to tell me how to set Harold straight."

"I am sorry, Marion," Tammy said. "I keep telling you that neither me, nor Chloe, is the answer to your marriage or any other problem that you may experience. Jesus is."

Marion said, "Well, then, Chloe it is. I will catch you later."

"Okay, Marion, take it easy and have a blessed day."

"I don't understand this," Tammy said after Marion hung up.

Those two are always having issues. It is one thing after the other. I can't understand why after all these years together that they can't decide if they should stay together or leave each other. Harold and Marion managed to live separate lives under the same roof. They were disrespectful to each other and were just plain abusive. No matter how hard I tried to get them to come to church with Eric and I, it never worked, but I keep praying that one day they will both find time for God and see the change it will bring to their lives, but they claim to have too much going on and cannot find the time to come to church with us, which I know is just an excuse.

Marion and Tammy were friends at Columbia College in New York, and they became reacquainted through a friendship that developed between Eric and Harold many years ago at the golf club. Tammy realized back then that Marion was still the same fun person and still had no desire to accept God into her life, but that did not prevent Tammy from becoming very close friends with Marion again. Marion was really fun to be with, and over the years she proved to be a really good friend to Tammy. It was during one of their nightly chats that Marion asked Tammy if she remembered Chloe, and Tammy said she did. Who could forget Chloe? Chloe was such a character in college. Marion, Chloe, and Tammy were in college together and Marion told Tammy that she had kept in touch with Chloe over the years and that she was not living far away and offered to arrange for a reunion, which turned out to be just like old times. From that moment on Tammy was always sandwiched between the Marion and Chloe. Marion always needed rescuing from her turbulent relationship with her husband Harold and Chloe...

Oh, time will not allow me to tell you all about Chloe, Tammy said. I seem to be a friend of sinners and unbelievers, but it was all good. I believe God's Word—that he came to save that which was lost, and that we all are vessels in his kingdom, and I believe God brought Chloe and Marion back into my life to help them.

Marion, Chloe and Tammy were not bound by their beliefs but by a unique kindred spirit—they loved each other for who they were. Chloe was an atheist; she did not grow up in a Christian home like Tammy did, and she never attended church, but she was surprisingly curious about Tammy's faith.

Chloe was always questioning Tammy as to why she could not do this or that, or challenging her as to why she could not go here or there, or why she especially made time to pray to someone she could not see. Tammy tried to help her understand by explaining to her that even though she could not see God, that she was always in his presence. Tammy further explained to Chloe that when she became a Christian, she no longer was a slave to sin, and God became her first priority; that some things and places were no longer appealing to her. But even though there were some places she didn't go or things she didn't do, Tammy told Chloe that she would always find time to spend with her.

Tammy's hope was that one day Chloe would come to understand just how good her God really is. But in the meantime, she would just remain persistent in her beliefs, to be patient and forgiving with her, and continue to show her by her conduct and in conversations with her about how Christianity had impacted her life in positive ways. However, she was concerned about Chloe's salvation. She could only pray for her and wait for the changes to take place in her life. She was praying that God would order Chloe's unruly mind and enter into her heart and give her a brand-new start.

From the time they met in college, Chloe was always the odd one out, but she was always fun to be around. She was frivolous at best and took life one day at a time. Chloe always maintained that she would never get married, or have children which would never fit into the life she was living, and her favorite saying was, "What's not broke, don't fix it." Chloe was a free spirit, and a gambler, in every sense of the word. She would always try to get Marion and Tammy involved in her get-rich-quick schemes, which always failed.

The latest one she was experimenting with was "rent a husband/wife," with more focus on the male species. Chloe's concept was that if you needed a father to go to your child's parent-teacher meeting or baseball game and you would not want to be the odd one out, you could rent one. If you had to go to a function and you didn't want to be a third wheel, you could rent a husband or wife for the event. But Chloe was doing more business renting husbands, and she was even borrowing them at times, skimming off the profits as Marion once told her.

In the past, Marion and Tammy had been cushions for Chloe to fall back on when her schemes went bust, but this one seemed to have promise, as there were so many single women who were fast becoming Chloe's customers. Every day Chloe seemed to manufacture another reason why one could rent a husband or wife, thus keeping her client list growing.

They would tease Marion about renting a husband from Chloe, since she seemed so unhappy with Harold, but they both knew that Marion was blessed in that department. She had the brains and the figure and the face to attract whomever she wanted. They always wondered why she married and stayed with Harold, even though they already knew the answer – Harold's money. But, they also knew that money did not and could not buy happiness, and Tammy hoped that one day Marion would understand this.

Chloe and Marion were always saying that Tammy was lucky to have a good life, but she kept telling them that she was not lucky, that she was blessed with a good life. They didn't think that she understood what they were going through at times, that she had never experienced some of the same things they did. But she did, and she would tell them one day. She would try, even though they would think that she was crazy. Tammy tried to explain to them before that she was living this life because she chose to live a God-dependent life and that she was given a second chance to be born again, to be spiritually born again into the family of God. She trusted God for everything. She prayed to God about everything. And her hope was that one day they would decide to take a stand for God and just taste and see that the Lord is good. For as long as they had been friends, Tammy was yet to convince them that living daily for God had great rewards, and she got the same answer from them every time she asked: "Is there any time left for God?" *Soon.*

Tammy knew that they told her this to get her to stop asking. They had been friends for so long that they were comfortable telling each other anything. Before, when Tammy would ask this of them, they would be so hostile that she was afraid to talk about God in their presence, but not anymore. Lately, Chloe and Tammy were always going at it respectfully, while Marion looked on as Chloe challenged the reasons for her belief, and sometimes, Tammy thought Chloe understood her reasoning but just wanted to provoke her.

Marion is definitely going through some changes. One moment she would be ranting and raving about Harold like today, and at other times she would be really mellow. Just last week she told me that she was ready for a change but was still not sure what she should do. Marion said the situation with Harold was wearing her down, but she still could not decide what to do. Tammy viewed this as work in progress. Marion probably thought Tammy didn't notice how keenly she now listened while she prayed for her, or hear her using her phases because she didn't comment. Marion especially liked to say, "Lord, have mercy on me," and then laugh out loud. And the questions she had been asking Tammy recently were all evidence that she was coming around. Tammy knew that in God's own time he would bring her into the fold. Marion might think that it was just a phrase, but God was listening, and Tammy knew he would be merciful to her.

Tammy didn't know if she would be able to ever make a believer out of Chloe, as she always had a reason to explain everything that happened under the sun. But Tammy vowed not to give up. The good thing was that Chloe was at a point where she no longer blocked her ears when Tammy prayed for her, and Marion no longer told her to talk to the hand. So Tammy promised herself that she would continue to allow God to work on them through her.

CHAPTER 6

Chloe's phone rang, and she answered. It was Marion in one of her mixed up moods.

"Chloe, where are you? Do you have time for breakfast?" Marion yelled on the other end.

"Sure, if you are paying," Chloe said.

"Girl, I'd pay even a door post to listen to me right now," Marion said.

"Well, Marion, you know I never pass up a free meal or good gossip, and I am sure this is what this breakfast is all about, right? Is Tammy joining us?"

"I think not," Marion replied. "Miss High and Mighty just blew me off, and you know when she starts down that Holy Ghost road I am jumping tracks. Just because she got the perfect husband, the perfect job, a perfect marriage, and everything else perfect, she thinks she can laud it over us. Well, today I need a friend who will understand me."

Chloe thought, *You mean a friend who is afraid to tell you like it is like Tammy would?* But she let Marion rant on as always and then asked, "So where are we having breakfast?"

"Sunny Side Up," she said.

"Okay, see you in fifteen minutes," and Chloe clicked off.

As Chloe was driving to meet Marion, she could not help but reflect on the conversation they just had. What Marion said about Tammy was not true or right, and she was too weak to stand up for her friend or to tell her other friend that if she was so dissatisfied with her life to do something about it. Maybe one day, she would get enough courage to say that. She really should. Tammy always credited her good life to God. Tammy was always praying for them, even though they didn't pray for themselves. Chloe didn't even know why she bothered, as she knew they were not interested in her prayers. Being a Christian had never prevented Tammy from being their friend, and a true friend she was. Marion hated it when Tammy set them straight, but Tammy was always right, and she did it in a nice way, not demeaning or condescending or proud, as Marion thought. She was just upset with Harold and could not help herself today, so it would all be forgiven.

Yes, Chloe the atheist knows all about forgiveness. Chloe said she had heard enough and seen enough from Tammy, but just didn't think she was ready or ever would be crazy enough to go all the way like Tammy did, turning the other cheek when people were unkind to her. Chloe believed in an eye for an eye. Chloe said Tammy was the most forgiving person she had ever met. Tammy once told them that unforgiveness always breeds evil and that she wanted no part of it, and tried to live peaceably with all men, but with me, there is another definition for peace.

Tammy once prayed for all stumbling blocks to be removed from her business when it was about to fail and asked her to forgive the person who was trying to shut her down. Chloe thought Tammy was going out of her mind. Tammy even told Chloe to try Jesus when everything else failed. But maybe if she failed a few more times and could not justify it, she might consider listening to Tammy's words that were always in the back of her mind: "Chloe, if all else fails, try Jesus. You can do all things through Christ because he strengthens you."

Chloe said she heard Tammy, but she knew that her strength came from the food she ate, and right now she needed to be at Sunny Side Up for her friend and enjoying Harold's money, and we all knew he had lots of it.

If Marion was not her friend, Chloe said she would befriend Harold too. She knew she could never say that in front of Tammy. She could hear her response already. "Chloe, all that glitters is not gold, and you should lust after things that will last, like God's love and his mercy."

She knew it sounded bad, but the truth was, right now she was lusting after the Spanish omelet at Sunny Side Up and a heaping cup of hot chocolate with whipped cream, pancakes with warm strawberry syrup, and whole, fresh strawberries on the side. She knew that she could not afford to eat like that every day, so if it meant that she had to endure Marion's ranting and raving while she enjoyed some good food, she'd live.

Marion was alright, but sometimes Chloe thought about what Tammy said, that Marion should be grateful rather than always complaining about Harold. Chloe kept telling her that all Harold needed was an occasional hug and a little time here and there to keep him happy, but Marion wanted the gifts but didn't want to appreciate the giver, which, coming from me Chloe, could be taken any way, but it was plain wrong. But who was she to judge; knowing that if the same situation was presented to her, she would not hesitate to take advantage of it. So she would let Marion off.

Chloe said she had been dating all the wrong men for all the wrong reasons, or as Tammy put it, they were always unevenly yoked, whatever that meant. Tammy said she should ask God for the things she needed, but Chloe said she would rather ask someone whom she could see and look straight into his or her eyes and know when they were trying to pull a fast one over her. If she should take Tammy's advise, and pray, that would mean she would have to wait, not knowing if she would meet God's approval, which she doubted she ever would, given the life she lived.

But according to Tammy, God heard and answered every prayer and that she only needed to ask and wait patiently for the answer. Tammy could say that, if she asked and God did not grant the request then she could always ask Eric. Chloe, on the other hand, said she knew that she would be back to square one.

Well, enough of that for today, this is getting too deep for me. Right now I need to be a friend to my friend and eat some good food for a change.

Chloe saw Marion's car as she was just pulling into the parking lot at Sunny Side Up. She pulled up beside

Marion's new Lexus, which made her little Betsy look really shabby. Marion waved at her and pulled all of her six feet, one hundred and eighty pound beautiful frame, outfitted like a Prima Donna out of the car.

Chloe just smiled and thought, *Mmmm, girlfriend sure knows how to live life. Now that is what I call living the abundant life, despite what Tammy says.*

They embraced each other, and Marion stepped back to look Chloe over.

"You know, girlfriend, you need a makeover." Then before Chloe could respond, Marion rocked back, laughing, and said," I mean make *me* over, Chloe, you look too good."

They laughed then hugged each other and entered Sunny Side Up together.

As the maître d' showed them to their table, he waited until they were seated then asked if they would like to start with their freshly squeezed orange juice.

"How about if I squeezed you?" Chloe asked.

"Chloe, be nice!" Marion said, then turned to the maître d' and said, "Yes, thank you. I would love a glass of orange juice please."

Marion turned to ask Chloe if she wanted the same thing, but Chloe already had her menu imprinted on her lips, and it rolled off.

"I'd like hot chocolate with whipped cream, pancakes with warm strawberry syrup, and whole, fresh strawberries on the side and a Spanish omelet."

Marion and the maître d started laughing at the same time, and Chloe said, "What? Is there a problem?"

The maître d just smiled, and said, "Coming right up!"

"Chloe!" Marion said. "Did you go to sleep last night dreaming of this food?"

"No, girl, I knew what I was craving but could not treat myself to it, so thank you, my friend. So talk to me. Let's dissect your new situation limb by limb."

Marion, after recalling the morning's event between Harold and herself, asked Chloe what she thought she should do. Chloe realized that her friend trusted her to be honest with her, and she told her exactly what she was thinking.

"Marion! You are my friend, right?"

"Yes, Chloe, you are my friend."

"Okay, if I was in a bad relationship and it was hurting me, would you encourage me to stay?"

"No," Marion said.

"Well, to be honest, from what I have seen between you and Harold, I think the relationship has run its course. You admitted to me today that you were thinking of killing Harold, and that is where you draw the line. You are a very smart, beautiful woman. With all your education and your fabulous body you could start over and be happier than you are today without Harold.

"Look at me, Marion, I have never been married. I have been in relationships, yes, and I know when to walk away, and sometimes maybe I run too soon. But my thing is, I don't want to wait around until things get sour. I prefer to get out while the going is good. It has worked against me more times than I could count, but at least I still have my self-respect, and I don't plan on going to jail for any man. It's just not worth it. So, you asked me, and I think I have been honest with you, but only you can make the ultimate decision. Only you can know when you have had enough.

"But come on. Is it worth it to be ridiculed, verbally and physically and abused by a man because of what he could give you? It all amounts to nothing if it's eroding your self-esteem. You are living a lie if you have to pretend with your friends that all is well and you are living in hell. Come on, Marion. I love you, and I know that I am not as savvy as you are, but please take my advice and look after yourself. I am sure that if you talk to Tammy she would put a different spin on this, but it would amount to the same. Get rid of the looser."

Chloe had never seen Marion cry, and by this time her friend was in tears, and she felt bad, but she asked her to be honest with her, and that is what she did.

Marion reached across the table, and she held Chloe's hand and said through her tears, "Thank you."

"I wish I had said something sooner."

"I am really going to think about what you said."

"Are you okay going to work today?" Chloe asked her.

"Yes." Marion said.

Chloe had to work also, so they hugged and said good-bye.

As Chloe pulled out of the parking lot, she looked in her rearview mirror, and Marion's Lexus was still parked where it was. She backed up to see if she was all right, and Marion was just hunched over her steering wheel crying. Chloe honked her horn, and when Marion looked at her, she was looking so distraught, she got scared. This was the second time Chloe had ever seen Marion like this, and she knew something was terribly wrong. Her first instinct told her to call Tammy, who knew how to fix everything, but she was not sure how comfortable Marion would be with this, so she decided she would ask her. Chloe got out of her car and opened Marion's door, and as she did, Marion broke down in sobs.

"Marion, I don't know what's going on, but I think you need someone other than me right now, so we need to call Tammy. Can I? Better yet, why don't you leave your car here and drive with me to Tammy's house, and she can meet us there."

Chloe was shocked when she nodded in agreement, but she was too scared to respond other than to help Marion out of her car. She was expecting just the opposite. When Chloe got her seated in her car, she called Tammy and explained to her that they needed her and would meet her at her house, and being the true friend that she was, she did not ask me any questions but said she would leave right away.

Chloe could not help but think about Tammy and the many times she asked them to attend church with her or go with her to the soup kitchen, and they always had an excuse why they couldn't, but yet whenever they needed her, she was always there. Chloe thought about what Tammy said to her one day after she had turned her down yet again was. "No matter how many times we reject God, when we need him, he is always there." It was like she was saying to Chloe, "You are always too busy when I ask you to do something with me, but when you need me, I am always there." Is that what Tammy called a conscience? Well, if that was the case, Chloe's conscience was definitely getting the better of her this morning.

She was just turning into Tammy's driveway when Marion said, "I should let you turn back."

"Why?" Chloe asked.

"I was just thinking through my sadness that no matter what we need or when we need it, Tammy is always there for us. We've turned her down so many times when she asks us to go to church or any other church function with her. I am feeling so guilty that all I ever do for her is to lay my burdens on her."

"Come on, Marion," Chloe said. "You know she does not think like that."

"I would," said Marion.

"Well, do you remember what she said to us when she tried to explain this Christian thing?" Chloe asked. "Tammy said that being a Christian means that sometimes one had to lay their own troubles aside and carry the cross of their brothers and sisters, just as Christ did. Tammy also said that we have to be there for each other, comfort each another, and encourage each another. Well, I never thought I would say this, but Tammy is right. This sounds fair.

"Maybe one day we should surprise her and go to church with her and just be there for her, as she does not ask much of us. And I am curious to see for myself just what is so special about going to church and the God she talks about so much and who she claims is doing so much for her. The more she talks about her church family and how they help each other, the more unreal it seems. I find it hard to believe that people really treat people so kindly in this world."

"Yes, they do, Chloe. Look at what you are doing for me, and you are not a Christian. Look what you did for me today," Marion said. "You dropped everything to make sure that I was okay. I feel so good just being here with you, Chloe. Thank you for being my friend. Today I really understand what true friendship really means, and I hate to admit it, but Tammy was right all along. As friends we have to lay aside our own troubles and help someone else. I really should be there for her more."

Chloe felt comfortable enough to tell Marion that she was thinking about pretty much the same things she just said.

"Marion," Chloe said, "Are we getting soft or what?"

"I don't know about you, Chloe, but Tammy is wearing me down with all this talk about Christianity and God, and for some reason, she always comes out on top. I don't know what to do."

"Take my advice, Marion. Continue doing what you have been doing all your life if it works for you. Like I always say, what's not broke, don't fix it."

At that moment Tammy pulled up alongside them in the driveway, jumped out of her car, and headed straight for them.

Chloe and Marion were already getting out of the car, and she said to them playfully, "Who needs the police or the ambulance? "We're good." Chloe answered, and

Tammy said, "I don't think so," but without questioning them further, Tammy said, "Let's go inside."

When they got inside, Tammy immediately went and turned on the coffee pot and went about getting them comfortable as if they were there for a therapy session, which was in fact exactly what they were there for. When she brought them the coffee mugs, she then asked what was wrong, and the therapy session started.

— ◆ —

As Marion recounted what had happened, Tammy noticed that Chloe seemed shocked but not overly alarmed and was not looking straight at her. Tammy was listening intently to Marion. Then, ever so gently, Tammy pulled up an ottoman in front of Marion, and holding her hands, she said, "Marion, do you want me to be honest with you?"

"Yes, Tammy."

Marion thought that she was going to start preaching to her, but instead she asked her if she was happy. Marion said no. She asked Marion if she loved Harold, and she said no. She asked if Marion wanted to go on living this lie, and she said no.

Then she asked, "What are you going to do?"

"I don't know."

Chloe, who was really very quiet, suddenly got up and said to Marion, "You need to know and fast before something crazy happens. Harold seems so angry now there is no telling what he could do next."

Tammy then got up and started pacing the floor as if in deep thought. Then she stopped abruptly and asked Marion another question. "Why have you stayed with Harold all these years if you don't love him? And how much longer are you prepared to go on living like this?"

"I can't," Marion said.

"Well then," Tammy said, "you need to get some professional help. We will be with you every step of the way, but this is your call. You have to decide what you have to do, and we will support you. We are friends, and friends support each other. Do you feel safe to go home to Harold?"

Marion assured them that she was and that she would not bother going in to work today, but she would go and seek professional help. Chloe and Tammy offered to go with her, but Marion admitted that this was something she had to do on her own, and so she left with Chloe to go and get her car.

———— ·◆· ————

After Chloe and Marion left, Tammy decided to pray for her friend. "Dear Lord, I come before your presence to lift up my friend Marion and her husband, Harold, before you. Lord, this abusive relationship is not your will, so I am asking you to intervene to heal this broken relationship, and, dear Lord, I have one other request of you. Save them. Wash them in your cleansing blood and make them whiter than snow. And bind them together in love. Use this situation to bring them closer to you, in your mighty name I pray. Amen."

CHAPTER 7

Meanwhile, Harold had just returned from his morning jog and started his day as he did every day, in front of the computer with a cup of hazelnut coffee, a bagel with vegetable cream cheese, and a Danish pastry that he picked up on his way back from his daily run. Since his early retirement from his old company and starting his own consulting business, Harold would begin and end the day monitoring the stock market. Marion once told him that the stock market was his God, and it was one of the main reasons for the disconnection in their marriage.

Harold had been investing wisely. A former president for Bank International, Harold was experienced in financial investments and money laundering, and daily tracking and managing his investments, as well as for his clients, was what Harold really enjoyed. Harold was ten years older than Marion, who was twenty-nine when he first met her, and the age difference did not deter him from falling in love with her. It was at a social event held in celebration of the Bank's fiftieth anniversary. Marion was there as a representative for one of the bank's premier customers, Tomorrow's Investments. This company encouraged investing for tomorrow. As a matter of fact, their slogan was, "Invest wisely today, vest heavily tomorrow."

Marion was the executive assistant to the company president, Robert Powell, whom Harold had known for years. When Robert introduced Marion to Harold, he could not let go of her hand. Marion, he noticed, had a smile that would make any dentist proud to have her as a client; her teeth were the straightest and whitest he had ever seen. She was wearing a dress that accentuated all of her greatest assets in the right way, and her hair and make-up looked like she had just stepped out of a salon. Marion was what you would describe as classy.

Harold kept finding reasons all night to speak to Robert just to engage Marion in conversation. Throughout the night Marion proved to be a great conversationalist, smart, knowledgeable about her company and the world, a well-rounded woman. Harold could see why Robert had chosen to invite her to this invent. This woman was aware of the attention she was getting but was classy enough to be just as Harold thought initially, classy, taking everything and everyone in stride. Harold was taking notes. He watched her from the way she carefully questioned the server about the wine selection before dinner to how she sniffed and appreciated the servers' recommendation and the way she thanked him flirtatiously yet not too suggestively.

This woman is going places, she just does not know it yet, Harold had thought. *And I am ready to lead her. With my money and this smart, beautiful woman at my side, there is no end to where we could reach.* But what Harold did not know was that Robert could have come to the event alone but that Harold was being set up from the get go by Robert who had tried to get Marion to go out with him from the moment he hired her. She would have none of it, and in her words, "You don't play where you work." But she did tell him that she was single and was looking for a good man. When Robert asked her to define a good man, Marion had said, "A man with lots of money and who would not hesitate to lavish it on me."

So naturally, Robert then asked Marion what she had to bring to the table or what she planned to give this man in return, and he said Marion looked him straight in the eye and said, "I have given enough in my lifetime, from my father who abused me to the cousin who raped me, and it's now time for me to stand on the receiving end." Marion told Robert how she had to work hard to put herself through college and was smart enough to hang around friends who were going somewhere and were generous enough to let her tag along. She told him that she was just tired of the struggles of life on her own and just needed to get a good break so that she could make something of herself. Robert asked Marion what she wanted out of life, and she said she was not sure but that she would someday like to have a real family but needed to have fun before settling down.

Marion loved her job, and it showed. Robert could not have asked for a better assistant; she was on top of everything. So when the event came up, Marion asked Robert if he was going to have a date for the event, and he told her that he was going alone.

Marion then said to him, "Well, why not take me along? Maybe my ticket to the good life awaits."

Marion had asked Robert if he knew of any eligible men at the event, and he assured her that there would be and that he knew the perfect one for her—his friend Harold

Hence, the meeting with Harold and Marion at the function and arranged by Robert.

———◆◆◆———

Their meeting blossomed into a friendship that escalated to marriage in a matter of months. Harold was blown away by Marion's beauty, and Marion was captivated by Harold's wealth, and prestige, and they did not seem to care about the age difference. They both seemed to be happy—they were getting what they wanted from the relationship, but Harold became so obsessive that Marion found it very unattractive very fast, and very soon they were at odds with each other, it seemed, every day.

Harold by then was caught in a web of his own making. He loved being seen with Marion, and he needed her to be his host at his numerous get-togethers. Harold had lavished so much praise on his wife to his friends and associates that now that things were going South, he was ashamed to let anyone know just how bad the situation really was.

Imagine what they would think, he thought, *a man like me sleeping on the sofa and my beautiful wife hanging out with who knows and where, and doing what. I really love my wife, and many times I really thought of just moving into another bedroom, but that is not what I wanted or needed. I wanted my wife whom I love so much to be in my bed, but by sleeping on the sofa, at least I was close to her. It's sad, but I am hoping that one day things will change.*

It had been going on for years, this farce of a marriage between Harold and Marion. Harold loved Marion, so much so, that he became a control freak, which did not sit well with Marion, who became rebellious as a result.

Marion refused to share a bed with Harold and would do as she pleased, and this made Harold more determined to control her, but this just resulted in more fights and insults between them. The relationship had taken such a turn that Harold was constantly accusing Marion of cheating, and Marion had challenged him at one point to do the same if he felt that would make them even. Harold told Marion that he could have easily taken a mistress as he could afford one, but that he loved her and was hoping that things would change for them and that Marion would agree to start a family.

———

But with the unhappy situation at home with all the fighting and upheavals, starting a family was the farthest thing from Marion's mind. Many times unbeknown to Harold, she thought of leaving him and starting her own business, but the thought was daunting in many ways, and despite what Harold was thinking, when she was out with her friends, Marion never cheated on him but said that too was about to change if things did not change at home real soon. Marion's life with Harold was not all that she thought it would have been. It had become a nightmare.

———————

Meanwhile, Harold was doing some soul-searching of his own. He said he did not want a divorce. He just wanted his beautiful wife to love him. Harold decided then that he would try to be less controlling with Marion and see if things would change. Harold knew that his friends were whispering about their marriage, and God knows he would not survive the shame and hurt if Marion were to leave him for another man, and so he decided to try to be a better husband, but there was too much salt in the wound, that he wondered if Marion would ever forgive him, but despite all this, Harold was willing to try.

Harold and Marion were unevenly yoked in more ways than one. Harold was much older than Marion, who was an unbeliever, and who had married Harold for material benefits. Harold had worked hard to become successful, and he wanted a beautiful woman on his arm as icing on the cake. Harold grew up in a Christian home, but when he left home for college, he stopped attending church, and when he started moving up the corporate ladder, he had even less time for God. Harold was too busy accumulating his massive wealth and doing whatever it took to make it, forgetting the moral values he was taught by his parents. All Harold cared about was making it to the top and making it good. But when Harold got to the top, when he thought he had it all, he was still lacking. He was lonely.

Harold then realized and acknowledged that he needed God back in his life and had started to attend church services again. However, when he married Marion, he tried to get her to attend church with him, but each weekend Marion had another excuse why she could not attend, and this was creating a problem between Harold and Marion.

Harold knew that Marion was an unbeliever before he married her, but he was hoping that she would change when they got married. But each week when he would ask Marion to accompany him at church, she had another excuse. Harold kept going to church until he ran out of excuses when he was asked how his wife was and if she was going to come to church with him the next Sunday. Harold became so embarrassed that he stopped going to church altogether, which was probably for the best, as by then, every day, Sunday to Sunday, their home was a battlefield with one fight after the other. They were both growing further and further apart, with neither of them making any effort to change course. Harold's Sundays were now spent on the golf course, and Marion spent most of the day in bed then going out with her friends.

CHAPTER 8

Tammy had appointments all morning and just had a quick lunch before her one o'clock appointment. She sat at her desk, using the time before her client arrived to run though her to-do list for the weekend. Tammy had so much to do. She had to do laundry. There was dry cleaning to be picked up and shopping to be done for the church's food pantry. She had choir practice. She had to pick up and drop off her mother's weekly supplies. She had to visit Sister Marsh in the nursing home, among other things. Her intercom buzzed, and her assistant, Roxy, informed her that her client Maxwell Thompson had arrived, and she told her to send him in.

Tammy had only spoken to Maxwell Thompson on the phone once before, but her assistant had created a profile for him. Tammy gathered from this profile that he was a partner at the prestigious Maxwell, Markham, Mahoney, and Associates based in New York, that he was single, and he was thinking of buying a home in Florida. Tammy smiled when she read the profile question as to whether the new home he wanted to buy was going to be a retirement or summer home. Mr. Thompson had responded that at forty he was not yet thinking of retiring but more of settling down if he could find the right woman.

Tammy heard stories like this every day at work and thanked God that she was a saved and sanctified, happily married woman, because God knows that many times if she was not happily married, saved, and sanctified, she would have easily tempted fate and mixed business with pleasure, as though pleasure was her business, because the opportunities were certainly there. Tammy often recounted stories of other real estate professionals who had done so with serious consequences and knew it was not worth the risk.

The knock at the door interrupted Tammy's reverie. "Come in," she said.

At the turning of the door knob, Tammy stood up and came around her desk to greet Mr. Thompson, who quickly put her at ease by asking her to call him Max. Max deserved a thumbs up. This man was fine in every way, and he smelled so good. In a matter of seconds, Tammy had summed him up—from the tailored, dark blue Armani suit molded to fit his well over six foot frame to the beautiful shine of his Stacey Adam's shoes. He was wearing a solid sky blue shirt with a matching tie with stripes of navy and sky blue colors and a smile to match.

When he had extended his hand in greeting, Tammy saw that he boasted a pair of star-shaped cuff links that shone as brightly as his eyes. It took all the professional strength Tammy could muster to stay focused. Tammy had not been so taken in by a man since she met and fell in love with her husband.

After they had exchanged pleasantries, Tammy invited him to sit down, and based on the information in his profile, she went over with him again the specifics before inviting him to follow her to the preview room. This was where Tammy had prepared photos and slides of some homes that she thought he would like to look at and some that she had taken the liberty of scheduling for showing. The preview room was adjacent to Tammy's office, and she indicated that, and Max was on his feet in a flash and opening the door for her.

As Max held the door open for Tammy with his right hand, his left hand went to the small of her back to guide her, as if this was her first time going into this room. When Tammy felt his hand on her back, it sent shivers up and down her spine, and she quickly tried to mask it and turned around, intending to say thank you. But, Tammy, being a tall woman, was almost as tall as Max, and when she turned around to say thank you, she found herself almost lip to lip with Max's lips, some very luscious lips indeed. Tammy did not know what came over her, but she felt herself moving into Max, and as he was leaning into her, they shared a kiss that was so passionate and so unexpected that when they realized what was happening, they both jumped back at the same time apologetically.

Tammy tried to regain control of the situation by asking Max if he wanted a cup of coffee or a glass of water, and he said coffee would be fine. Tammy was glad to run from the room to regain her composure. Tammy was so ashamed of herself, but at the same time thought how much she enjoyed the kiss.

On returning to the room, she said. "Mr. Thompson, where were we?"

He looked at Tammy with the sweetest of smile and said, "I believe Mr. Thompson was my father, so please call me Max."

Tammy told Max that given what had just transpired she did not feel comfortable calling him Max. He then told her how very sorry he was and that it wouldn't happen again.

"I did not set out to make you uncomfortable or to put you in this awkward position, but it seemed like the chemistry between us was just too strong. If you would rather have one of your other associates continue for you, I would not oppose."

"Not at all," Tammy said, against her better judgment. "It is okay."

"Very well then," he said. "Shall we continue?"

Tammy and Max then looked at several of the photos of the houses. Then Tammy informed him that she had scheduled a few for showing to him, if he had the time, and he said that he had planned to stay the weekend and indeed had the time. Tammy then told him that he could ride with her in her car, and so they set off to view the first home on the list.

With Max being so close to Tammy in the car, his cologne was like an aphrodisiac. Tammy was feeling subconsciously high with animalistic thoughts going through her mind. She tried to bring herself back to the present when she realized that he had asked her a question.

"Pardon me," she said, and Max repeated his question about if she had any other clients scheduled for the day.

All the right senses told Tammy to say yes, but she heard herself say, "Oh no, I had pretty much freed up my schedule for you this afternoon."

Max said he felt honored and wanted to know if she did this often or just to certain clients, and knowing where her thoughts had been regarding the kiss, Tammy quickly came to the defensive and told him that she was a happily married woman who never mixed business with pleasure, if that's what he was thinking.

"Oh no," Max responded quickly, "I never meant it that way, and I am sorry."

Tammy said, "I don't know what came over me, responding to you like that."

"Tammy, allow me to explain what I meant," Max said. "I was thinking that if you went out of your way like this for all of your clients with the preparation and all that, no wonder your business is thriving so well."

"Oh!" Tammy said sheepishly. "I am sorry too. I don't always fly off the handle like that, but I have to admit, you really caught me off guard. Let's just try to put that awkward moment behind us."

Max put out his hand to shake on it, and as Tammy shook it his hand felt warm to the touch and sent chills through her. Tammy quickly pulled her hand away from his as if it was burned by hot coals, and she walked toward the window, trying to clear her mind to get back on track. When she felt in control again, Tammy told Max that she had one more house to show him. Tammy told him that the owners for this one had put the house on the market several times and then changed their minds but had since built a new home and once again put it back on the market.

"Well, what are we waiting for?" Max said. "Let's see this home before they change their minds again."

And off they went.

The rest of the day went very well, and as they were viewing the last house, Marion's phone rang. When she saw that it was Chloe, she said, "Excuse me, Max. This call will just take a minute."

Max told her that it was okay, and he would just continue to look around.

"Hey, Chloe, what's up?"

"I was just checking in with you to see what time you want to meet us for happy hour," Chloe responded.

"I am just showing my last house for the day to an out-of-town client, and we were just wrapping up. I will soon be there."

"Oh," Chloe added hastily, "I know that you usually take your out-of-town clients to dinner. Are you going to take this one to dinner?"

"I was planning to, but since we spent more time that we originally planned for, I don't think he has the time to go to dinner, and if we do, I will be very late catching up with you and Marion."

"Well, maybe you could have your client join us as it is Friday. You said it was a man, right?"

"Affirmative," Tammy said.

"After all, if he is thinking of buying a house in Florida, he needs to see how we rock it on a Friday after a hard day's work." Chloe said.

"You know I don't mix business with pleasure, Chloe."

"Come on, Tammy," Chloe said. "Don't be such a straight lace. It's Friday, and who knows, he may be the Mister Right I am searching for."

"Okay, okay, but just this once," said Tammy. "I will ask him, but you have to promise to be on your best behavior."

Tammy knew that Max had heard most of the conversation, and when she asked him if he had plans for dinner, he said he needed to make a call first but would be delighted to have dinner with her. Tammy quickly explained to him that she usually meets her girlfriends for Happy Hour on Fridays and that they had suggested that she bring him along to familiarize him with Florida Fridays.

Tammy thought that the last thing she wanted to do was to be alone or in close proximity to Max after the brief kiss that they had shared. *I have enough demons on my back already, and I am still trying to work out the war that was raging in my mind regarding Max. But I am a professional after all, and a happily married woman at that. It was only a kiss, and it will never happen again.*

With that mental boost, Tammy gave Chloe the answer she was hoping for, and they spoke for a few minutes more before ending the call.

Max had stepped out of the room to make his call, and Tammy's heart rate was slowly returning to normal. She was thinking of Eric and what he would think of her after what she had done today. Tammy's heart rate started rising again as she immediately started battling with her conscience. *Should I just confess my wrong doing to God and keep this secret to myself, or if this burden gets too heavy, can I trust one of my girlfriends? But, which one?*

Tammy then called out to Max to see where he was, and he called out that he was in the master bedroom. When Tammy entered the room, Max was standing at the window, enjoying the view, and he beckoned for her to come and look.

As she stood next to him, Max turned to Tammy with a gleam in his eyes and said excitedly, "I think this is the house for me."

Tammy asked him how he knew, and he said he felt it, and as he said so, he reached out and hugged Tammy saying, "Thank you."

Before Tammy could respond, they found themselves wrapped in yet another embrace and kissing each other hungrily, and when they moved away from the window, they both fell back onto the bed. They were thrown together as if with the force of hurricane winds and held on to each other as if clinging for dear life, not wanting to let go, and they made love with a fierceness, an urgency that left them breathless. Tammy and Max were exhausted, and they hugged each other and fell asleep in each other's arms.

About an hour later, it was the ringing of Tammy's phone that jolted them awake. It was Chloe again asking where she was. Tammy was now wide awake, and not knowing how to answer, she fumbled on her words. Chloe picked up on this and asked if she was okay. Tammy quickly tried to regain her composure and told

Chloe that they were running a bit late but that they would soon be there.

When she turned around, Max was just looking at her pretty much the same way that Eric looked at her after they were intimate, and immediately the guilt and shame washed over her, and she started to cry. Max tried to reach out to comfort her, and she pushed him away. He looked so hurt, and Tammy felt so dirty that she scrambled for her clothes and ran to the bathroom. Tammy did not care that she was not supposed to be using the shower, but she scrubbed and scrubbed her body, as if trying to erase Max's touch. Tammy wished she could stay in the bathroom and never come out.

As she emerged from the bathroom, Max said to her, "Tammy, I am sorry, not for making love to you, but for placing you in this position knowing that you are married, but I just could not help myself. I will not apologize for loving someone as beautiful as you. I felt something for you so strong, and I know you felt it too—"

"Stop! Stop it!" Tammy shouted. "I feel dirty, cheap, dishonest, and broken, and I...and I don't know what I am going to do now. How am I going to go home and face my husband, who has been everything to me? Oh, dear God!" Tammy shouted. "I am supposed to be meeting my friends. What am I going to do? I am mess. I can't let them see me like this. How would I explain this? I can't go home to my husband, because I can't face him, knowing what I have done."

Tammy remembered that she had promised to bring Max with her to happy hour with Chloe and Marion and wondered how she was going to do this.

I cannot get over myself. I can't understand what came over me to do something so Chloe, so crazy. Now, how am I to ever judge Chloe again for her wild ways when I was just the same, only crazier, because I was married to the most wonderful man on the planet whom I adored? We never keep secrets from each other. Now, how am I supposed to live with this on my conscience? How am I supposed to kiss my husband again or make love to him without thinking about what happened today? What if became pregnant? I need to pray.

Lord, please forgive me for my moment of weakness, for allowing my sinful nature to surface and control me. Lord, I know that I am not perfect, but I also know right from wrong. Why did I allow myself to be weak? Why was I attracted to this man, this stranger? Is something wrong in my marriage? Am I not as happy as I thought I was? Lord, I know that I could depend on you to make every path smooth and every crooked way straight. You alone could lift up the fallen and help them to stand, and I need your help this day. Show me the way out of this dreadful situation, and Lord, help me never to allow the desires of my heart to lead me into temptation and fall into sin. This is my prayer, in Jesus's name.

As Tammy finished her confession, Max was just standing there, as if he was not sure what to do with himself.

Tammy said, "No need to prolong this. Let's go. If you don't feel up to meeting with my friends, I will be happy to make an excuse for you and one for myself. I will just make a call and let them know that I was running later than usual, as the client decided on the house, and there was paperwork to begin before he went back to New York."

Max agreed that this was probably for the best.

Tammy called Chloe then conferenced-in Marion and told them that her meeting with her client was running late and as a result had to cancel on them.

Marion, always as sharp as ever, asked, "Is everything all right?"

Tammy assured her that all was well but that they were running a bit late and did not want to be too late and ruin their plans. This was not totally the truth. The fact was, Tammy was scared of being around Max after what they had done and afraid that her friends would see right through her.

Marion and Chloe were not about to let her off that easily. Marion accused her of bailing on them, and Chloe accused her of trying to block her from meeting her future Mister Right. At that Tammy had no choice then but to let them know that they would be there. I will call you when we are on our way. That settled, they said good-bye and hung up.

As Tammy did so, Max asked her if everything was okay. She told him that her friends refused to take no for an answer and that they would meet them at Casa Cassaria.

Max said, "Sounds like a plan, Tammy, but I would understand if you could not work with me anymore after today."

They both agreed that another associate should take over and conclude the sale of the house and that they would try to forget everything that happened today.

It was easy for Max to say and do, Tammy thought, *as he did not have a wife to go home to. I, on the other hand, don't know how I will ever live this down. I have fallen so low. I don't know how or if I could ever be the same person again. I was a hypocrite, a thief, and a cheater—a slut.*

Max and Tammy drove back to the office in silence. They quickly signed the temporary offer to purchase agreement, and then Tammy assigned him to someone else to conclude the sale. They left the office and started walking toward Tammy's car, but Max hurried along in front of her and was already opening the driver's door to let her in. As he helped her into the car, his arm brushed against Tammy's breast, and he embarrassingly turned around to apologize, and again they were in each other's arms kissing.

When they broke away again, apologetically, Tammy said, "I don't think dinner is a good idea. I should go home."

"But what would you say to your friends?" Max asked.

"You are right. They will have questions that I am not prepared to answer, so I will drive ahead of you, and this cannot happen again. I don't know what is wrong with me today. I have never behaved in this manner before."

"It must be chemistry, as I can't seem to help myself." Max replied.

Max again started to help Tammy into her car, and she politely said, "No, thank you." Tammy then settled herself into her seat and just sat in the car with the engine idle, watching Max in her rearview mirror until he returned to his car to follow her to the restaurant. She then called Chloe to let her know that they were on their way to meet them.

———◆———

Max went back to his car, and as he watched Tammy drive off, he thought, *what a beautiful woman! I don't know how I am ever going to ever forget this day or this woman. I am a man but not one who usually gets caught up in the moment or behaves recklessly, but this was just different. It was like nothing I have ever felt for any woman before. How I would love to come home to her every night to just hold her in my arms and tell her all about my day and listen to her tell me about her day. Atta boy, one more bad move, and you will have to call one of your friends to defend you from a sexual harassment law suit. But Tammy just seems so well put together. I'd have to be blind not to be attracted to her, and even for a blind man my animalistic instincts would draw me to her. Yes, she is that type of a woman.*

Max was tempted to call his best buddy to tell him about his realtor but thought against it. *Man, this is something I have to take to my grave or it could come back to haunt me. I should know. I have seen this too many times in the court room.*

So Max just turned on the radio in the car and tried to focus on following Tammy to the restaurant, and that's when a Whitney Houston song came on, "I will always love you." And this song told him what he needed to do, exactly what he had to do…

If I should stay,

I would only be in your way.

So I'll go, but I know

I'll think of you ev'ry step of the way.

And I will always love you.

I will always love you.

You, my darling you. Hmm.

Bittersweet memories

that is all I'm taking with me.

So, good-bye. Please, don't cry.

We both know I'm not what you, you need.

When the song ended, Max could not believe what had just happened. Had ill fate just dismissed him like that?

CHAPTER 9

When Max and Tammy got to the café, Marion and Chloe were nowhere in sight, so they went in together.

Max flashed the maître d a bright smile, and they exchanged pleasantries before she asked Max, "Table for two?"

Max then looked at Tammy questioningly, and she said, "No, table for four, thank you. "We are going to be joined by two of my friends, Chloe and Marion."

She led them to a table in the far corner and asked if the table was okay and if they wanted to order any cocktails before the other members of the party arrived. Max said, yes, and the maître d gave them the drinks menu.

"Your waitress will be right over to take your orders."

When the waitress arrived, Tammy ordered a bottle of sparkling water, and Max ordered a glass of Chardonnay.

To try to make pleasant conversation, Tammy then asked Max if he had other plans for the weekend. Max said he always loved coming down to Miami and that he planned to use the time to unwind before going back to his crazy schedule on Monday.

At that moment, as if riding on the tail end of a hurricane, Chloe breezed in. She stooped to kiss Tammy.

Then before Tammy could introduce her to Max, who was already standing, pulling out a chair for Chloe,

Chloe, just being her usual self, exclaimed, "Am I on a GQ set or what! Because I am looking at poster boy of the year!"

"Chloe!" Tammy interrupted. "Please meet my client Maxwell Thompson."

"Call me Max," he said to Chloe.

"Maxwell! You are maxing well indeed."

"Thank you," he said in response with a smile as bright as the sun, obviously enjoying Chloe's banter. He gestured for Chloe to sit, and he adjusted her chair before seating himself again. Then he signaled for the waitress.

"So, what are you having, Chloe?" Max asked.

"Do I have a choice?" she asked.

"We all have choices," Max said.

"Well, in that case, where do you fall on the menu?"

Max started rolling out of his chair with laughter.

"Chloe!" Tammy said. "He asked what you wanted to drink not eat."

Not waiting for Chloe to respond, Max asked, "Where do you want me to fall, Chloe?"

"Well," Chloe said, "if I really had a choice, you would be my aphrodisiac first, then appetizer, soup, salad, entrée, dessert, and a night cap in that particular order."

"Chloe!" Tammy interjected. "I thought I asked you to be on your best behavior."

"I am so sorry, Tammy," she said. "I am trying, but it is not easy. Max, I am sorry, but you seem like the closest thing to heaven this side of earth. I am sure you hear this every day."

"Well, that is partly true," Max replied, "but not from someone as beautiful as you are."

"Okay, you two," Tammy said, "you have company, remember?"

With that they both laughed and in stepped the diva herself, Miss Marion.

"Well, hello there! What have we got here? Am I at the right table or what? Well, allow me to introduce myself. I am Marion, and you must be Maxwell."

"Mr. Thompson to you," Chloe said sharply, "and it would be nice if you could be on your best behavior."

Both Tammy and Marion looked around the room and back again, as if looking for the person who spoke.

"That could not be Chloe's voice we just heard," Tammy said.

Max broke out laughing. He said, "This is truly a good start to what I can see is going to be a wonderful weekend."

The waitress appeared as if on cue and asked for their orders.

"Well, ladies," Max said, "since this is your favorite spot, could I trust one of you to order for me?"

"Do we need to draw lots?" Chloe asked.

They all started laughing. It was well after 9:00 p.m. when Tammy said she was tired and was ready to leave. Marion too decided to call it a night after the next drink, but Chloe, as usual, teased them, calling them old married ladies and told them she would treat Max to some good ole Miami hospitality since the party poopers were going home.

Max stood up as Tammy got up to leave and shook Tammy's hand, thanking her for the day and saying that he would be in touch soon. He then asked Tammy if he could see her safely to her car. Tammy, not trusting herself to be with Max after what had happened earlier today, told Max that it was okay, but Max insisted that it was the gentlemanly thing to do, so Tammy bid them goodnight and walked over to Max, who took her hand, and they left.

"Mmmmm," Marion muttered as they were leaving. "Oh, Chloe, I should be going home to a man like that, not that Harold who is no doubt waiting at home to give me grief."

"Girl, count your blessings," Chloe said. "The grass always looks greener on the other side. You told me something like that not so long ago. A man as fine looking as Max probably sleeps with a different woman every night."

"I know," Marion said, "but I am so very tired of Harold's possessiveness, his moodiness, and his everythingness. I just wish I had a rock solid marriage as Tammy and Eric's."

<hr>

At that point, Tammy and Max reached her car, and as she turned around to say good night, they were again locked in another embrace and kissing ever so passionately. The happily married, saved, and sanctified Tammy, the same Tammy who did not mix business with pleasure, had acted inappropriately—and with a stranger, no less, and now she was battling with her conscience to go home and face her husband.

They both again started apologizing at the same time, and with tears in her eyes, Tammy pulled away from Max, but Max reached out and held her face in both of his hands and said, "Tammy, I think I am in love with you, and I will always love you."

Tammy quickly pulled away, ran, and locked herself in her car, too shaken to drive away immediately, thinking that she felt something too—but love, no. *I am in love with my husband.* Tammy's thoughts immediately went to Eric, and shame overwhelmed her. How was she ever going to face him again? *Lord, help me. My marriage will never be the same again. I will never be the same again.*

CHAPTER 10

Tammy called Eric to see if he was home yet and to let him know that she was on her way home, but the call went to voicemail. Eric was a Life Coach at the boys club at the church. They met on Fridays after work, one of his many involvements in the church, and she was hoping that he would be late. Eric was usually home before her, and she knew that he would be running a bubble bath for the both of them and waiting for her with open arms, but tonight, she needed time to compose herself, to redeem herself, someway, somehow.

Tammy usually smiled at the thought of seeing her husband after a long day, but as she pulled into her spot in the two-car garage, her spirits fell when she saw Eric's car already in the garage, as guilt washed over here again.

What have you done? Tammy berated herself. *What is wrong with you? Okay, pull yourself together. You already confessed this to God. You promised not to do anything so stupid or reckless again, but it was wrong, so very wrong, but even though it was wrong, you are human, and humans make mistakes. Just learn from this.*

With that boost, Marion pulled herself up and out of her car, but before she could turn the key in lock, the door sprang open, and Eric was all over her.

"I missed you so much today, baby. I could not wait for you to get home. So, how was your day, sugar? Closed any big deals today?"

At the mention of deals, the incident with Max became front and center of Tammy's focus again. Tammy was tempted to just come clean and tell Eric of her mistake, but at the same time, it came to her. What would Eric have done? Would he have confessed to her? She made a decision then and there to try and forget it.

So she quickly turned the attention from herself by saying casually, "Friday's could be surprising, but not today, I am just tired. As she dropped her pocketbook on the counter she said, Now you tell me about your day."

Eric's firm had just finished the design for a massive low-income family complex, and he had been so excited about this. According to Eric, with all the construction going up and around them, the city of Miami was focused on boosting up the market for tourism, while the middle and lower class got pushed into the background. But with the election of the new mayor, the city had begun to experience changes that were long overdue and very welcomed.

Eric went on to explain that there were improvements being made to the parks, new bus shelters being installed, new schools being built, and now a complex for low-income families. This was all very welcoming, as with the decline in the job industry, the needs bracket was widening more and more each day.

Tammy was barely holding on to what Eric was saying and was glad that he had so much to say, because she did not know what to say to him. According to Eric, the recent economic downturn saw so many people out of jobs. More soup kitchens and food pantries were being opened. More families were facing foreclosure. Rentals had skyrocketed. They wondered just how much worse things would get before they got better, so any new development for the city was good news.

Eric went on to comment on how he so much applauded the Church of Promise's announcement, encouraging members to help the less fortunate in any way possible. It could be from car-pooling to sharing their groceries. Just last Sunday he recalled that while giving out the notices, Elder Thomas announced that a family who had just lost everything they owned in a fire was in need of a mattress, and that the requesting family was willing to take even an air bed and linens, and any used clothing for their children. Eric said every week it seemed like church members who were in better positions were becoming true ambassadors for Christ by lending, sharing, or helping those in need, and as the scriptures says, if you do this to the least of them, you are doing it unto the Lord.

Eric then told Tammy a story of one of the little boys in the club who had just informed them that his mother had left them, and that both him and his younger brother were now being taken care of by an aunt who already had four children of her own and an abusive husband. The boy said they were not sure how long they would be able to stay there, as their uncle kept asking their aunt when their druggy mother was coming to get them. He said their uncle was complaining that he did not sign up for feeding extra mouths, as he could barely take care of the ones he had. Eric recounted to Tammy that the boys were scared and that if their mother did not come back soon, their uncle would make good on his threat to call social services for them and have them sent to different homes.

Immediately, Tammy's heart went out to the boys, and she quickly pushed aside her guilt and asked Eric if there was anything that they could do to help. Eric asked her if she would agree to take the boys to stay with them temporarily should the uncle make good on his threat, and Tammy agreed.

Eric and Tammy had been trying for years to have children and were still waiting on the Lord to answer their prayers. In her daily petition to God, Tammy always recounted the story of Sarah who conceived when she was ninety years old and knew that her wait might seem long, but she was confident that if she was patient and believed, that God could turn any situation around for good to those who loved him. Tammy said she sure did love the Lord, despite her failures, and that Eric was always encouraging her to keep praying as he was for a son or a daughter.

Tammy and Eric were blessed in so many other ways that, according to Tammy, it was easy for them to keep on earnestly in prayer. It seemed like for every disappointment in their lives God rewarded them doubly in other areas, and that is why they were always finding time for God, because they were so thankful for all the many blessing he bestowed on them.

Tammy was always amazed how her friends that she love dearly would find time for everything and everyone else but never anytime for God, and she tried to encourage them to taste and to see how good God is. But she had yet to get a positive answer every time she asked the question, "Is there any time left for God?" Tammy made it a point to find time for God, because he had done so much for her, and his mercy and goodness toward her was never ending, and especially now she was asking for his forgiveness for her infidelity.

Tammy realized many, many, years ago when she was walking in darkness that without God she was nothing, but since she had been walking in his marvelous light, she was spending quality time in prayer with Him, helping others, attending church, visiting the sick and shut in— things that she did not have time to do when she was walking in darkness. Tammy continued to thank the Lord every day for showing her his marvelous light, but tonight she recognized the need for him to lift her up from the depths of her despair.

Tammy thought, *I don't know how I have fallen so low, but I know I serve a forgiving and an understanding God, a God of second chances who I know still loves me, even at this time when I am unlovely.*

"Earth to Tammy!" Eric said. "Where are you?"

Tammy shook herself back to the present and told Eric that she was reflecting on where God brought her from and was thanking him for all that he had done for her and for the many times that she had fallen and he had forgiven her, and today she was in dire need of his forgiveness for something terrible she had done and one that she shamefully had to admit to him and ask his forgiveness also.

"Eric," Tammy started, "please forgive me. I have done something so unlike me, so shameful that I don't know where to begin. I promise you, Eric, that something like this will never happen again," and with that she broke down and started crying.

Eric, now alarmed, came and hugged her, asking her what could be so wrong. Tammy then recounted what happened with Max, assuring him that this had never happened before in their marriage and that it was a moment of weakness. Tammy told Eric that she was not forced to sleep with Maxwell Thomson but that there was just the physical attraction between them that they both succumbed to.

Tammy had never seen this look on Eric's face in all the years they had been married—the hurt look. The disappointment was so evident that Tammy just wanted to crawl into a hole and die.

When Eric opened his mouth to speak, nothing came out, and when he tried again to speak, it was through clenched teeth. "How could you do this, Tammy? How could you do this to us? Have I ever cheated on you? Was I not enough man for you? Are you unhappy?"

"No, no, no, Eric," Tammy said. "We were intimate this morning, and we were so in love when we left home, and I still am, we still are. I don't know what to say. I just hope that you can find it in your heart to forgive me. I don't know, Eric. I don't know what came over me.

You are the best thing that ever happened to me, and you have been a good husband to me, a God-fearing man that I prayed for, and I am asking you to please forgive me, because I love you and want to spend the rest of my life with you.

"Eric, before I came home I prayed to God and asked for his forgiveness and was contemplating keeping it a secret, but knowing the agreement we made to never keep secrets from each other, I could not break this pact, and I am trusting that our love will cover my grave sin. Can you please forgive me?"

Eric did not say anything for a while. He just walked around the room, punching the air. Then he went to the kitchen, and he came back with a full bottle of wine, and putting it to his mouth, something Tammy had never seen him do, he drank two gulps.

Tammy was scared. She thought Eric was going to hit her, but instead Eric threw the bottle at the fireplace and went back to the kitchen and came back with yet another bottle of wine. He opened it, started to put the bottle to his mouth, then he brought it down with a thud on the table.

Tammy was too scared to speak. She wanted to get up and bolt for the door but was paralyzed with fear. When Eric turned again to pick up the bottle, Tammy knew that she had to do something, and she jumped up and grabbed his arm.

Eric just swung her around and said, "Leave me alone. I need to numb this pain I am feeling." Eric was trembling with rage and fear.

Marion didn't know how else to describe what she was seeing but was scared for Eric and for herself, and realizing the damage that she had caused, she started to cry again and could not stop.

When Tammy saw how hurt Eric was, her heart felt like someone had taken it out and was stomping on it. *Imagine what he must be feeling*, she thought. *Maybe, I should have kept quiet about this, but I know that I would not have been able to live with myself. Will I ever get past this? I am overwhelmed by my sorrows.*

Tammy then felt like vomiting and ran for the bathroom. Tammy was in the bathroom for a while when the thought came to her to drown herself in the bathtub. Tammy filled the tub with water, and when the tub was filled to the brim, she wrapped a towel around her head and slipped sideways into the tub. Tammy could not recall how long she lay in the tub, but she knew that she was too afraid to take her own life, so she just lay there drowning in her sorrows, and it was there that Eric came and found her.

Eric calmly pulled her up out of the water and wrapped a towel around her and helped her get dressed. When Tammy was dressed, she sat on the side of the bed and started crying again. Eric looked at her as though his heart was breaking, as if he had done something to make her cry, and this just made Tammy cry all the more.

"Come," Eric said. "We will put this to rest now. Let us pray.

Heavenly Father, I forgive Tammy as I would have wanted her to forgive me. I am not perfect, and we are human. We fall short, but knowing that you, our God, is a God of second chances, a God who will never turn his back on us, how could I not forgive her? I love Tammy enough to look beyond this. I can see this is tearing her apart, but I will always remember that even in our moments of weakness you love us still. Thank you, Jesus, for my wife's sincere heart to share this with me and trusting me to love her still, despite her fault. Continually bind us together in love and help us to be loving, kind, and true one to another always. Lord, when temptations arise, help us to boldly rebuke them in name of Jesus. Lord, your Word reminds us that whom you have joined together let no one put asunder. Your Word reminds us that love is patient, love is kind, love is forgiving, and love is true. And that love covers a multitude of sins. I believe in my heart that we have laid this tonight at your feet, and we trust you to cover us with your blood and wash away from us every stain of sin so that we may come before you with clean hands and pure hearts. In Jesus's name I pray, amen."

When Eric finished praying, Tammy was so touched. She was so ashamed, so relieved, and so thankful, that she was overwhelmed by her emotions and she began to cry and could not stop crying. Eric just hugged her tighter and made her promise to turn this client over to one of her associates. Tammy thanked Eric for forgiving her, for loving her despite her failure, and told him that she had already turned the client over to one of her associates.

Tammy felt like a great weight had been lifted off her chest, and said, "Thank you, God."

They both just sat there for what seemed like hours, just holding each other tight and not saying a word. Then Eric asked her if she was planning to drown herself in the bathtub earlier, and she told him yes, but that she could not go through with it and instead just lay in the tub, hoping to wash away all the troubles of the day.

As she said this to Eric a wave of apprehension came over her. O*h, dear Lord. What have I done? I slept with a man without protection, a man who was not my husband. What if I get pregnant? God, please don't let this happen, not now, not this way. Please.*

Eric must have felt something, because he just held her tighter and said, *"Let it go Tammy, let it go,"* and she *cried herself to sleep in his arms.*

CHAPTER 11

Meanwhile, Marion was just driving around, not wanting to go home to face another showdown with Harold, who had been calling her all day. It was getting late, and Marion was almost certain that Harold by this time would have already been to the clubhouse with his friends and would be steamed and ready for battle.

Marion parked the car in the garage and just sat there, contemplating if she should just sleep in the car. *I just can't go another round with Harold tonight*, she thought. *I am so very tired, tired of all this drama day after day, night after night. How much more of this can I take? I am at my wits end. When I left the house today, it was a war zone, and I am coming back home now to a battle field no doubt. It seems like I am only happy away from my home. I should just pack my stuff and leave Harold, but that would mean me paying rent and other bills that would force me to give up the luxuries I now enjoy being Harold's wife.*

But as Marion sat there pondering all these things, she began asking herself some serious questions. *How much longer can I go on living with this abusive man, and if I leave and have to give up the luxurious life, what would my friends think about me?*

Marion did not have the answers to these questions, and she was too ashamed to let her friends really know how bad things were at home and did not know how to ask for their help. Marion now realized that she was just living her life for others and playing a game of false pretences.

Even though Marion had confided in Tammy and Chloe, they did not know just how bad things had become, as each time they asked Marion pretended that all was well. But now Marion wondered what would happen if she was to really open up to her friends and let them know what she had been going through. Marion thought of what or how much she should tell her friends, and as she thought about it, she knew she had to tell them everything.

Marion could not lie anymore. She could no longer pretend to Tammy and Chloe that all was well. She would tell Chloe and Tammy the truth regarding her situation and not have them think that she was just going through another misunderstanding with Harold and wanted to leave.

I can just imagine what my friends would say if I did not tell them the whole truth. Chloe would want to know if I had lost my mind, thinking of leaving Harold and all the bling, bling she is so fascinated with, and Tammy would encourage me and tell me to give it over to God. I don't think I am ready for either one, so I guess I have to go inside to face Harold.

Marion was feeling suddenly very tired, and before she knew it, she had fallen asleep in the car, and there she slept for hours.

When Marion awoke, she was startled at first. Then remembering where she was, a sickening darkness engulfed her. Earlier when Marion had pulled into the driveway, she saw that the lights were on in the living room, which meant that Harold was either waiting up for her or had fallen asleep on the sofa; she was hoping for the latter. Marion turned the key in the lock quietly and entered into the foyer, but Harold was waiting for her.

He blocked her way, and he shouted, "Where are you coming from at two o'clock in the morning?"

Marion was still tired and was in no mood for a showdown and did not answer Harold and tried to slide past him, but Harold was already in full combat mode, and he swung Marion around by her arm and shouted again.

"Marion! I asked you where you are coming from at two o'clock in the morning!"

Marion said, "Harold, let go of my arm right now."

But instead of doing as she asked, Harold slapped her hard across her face. Marion staggered sideways from the impact and landed next to a table and held on to it to regain her balance. But before she could do so, Harold charged at her again, and as Marion tried to scramble away from him, Harold caught up with her in the living room, and he slapped her again, and this time Marion fell against the fireplace, hitting her head. When Marion lifted her hand to her head and took it away, it was covered with blood.

From the corner of Marion's rage-filled eyes, she saw the poker for the fireplace, and without thinking, she grabbed it and swung at Harold with all her might. The poker connected with the intended target—Harold's leg. And as he grabbed at his leg, Marion took another swing at him, this time higher. Marion was quickly regaining her composure and connected Harold another blow across his stomach, and she heard him gasp as though all the air in his lungs had escaped, and he fell, groaning.

Marion stood over Harold with the poker raised to strike him again, and through clenched teeth, said, "Don't you ever think of laying your filthy hands on me again. If you do, I will be prepared. If you catch me off guard, you had better be sure you kill me, because I will not hesitate to put you down for good. I am tired of your physical and verbal abuse, and tonight it stops here."

Harold looked up at Marion, either in too much pain or too shocked to speak, and Marion saw that he was bleeding from his leg and that he was still gasping for breath, but she brought down the poker hard and swift, once across his back, and again. This time it was a crushing blow to his right arm that he had slapped her with, and it left him bleeding. Marion ran and locked herself in the bathroom, where she sat propped up behind the door, trembling with fear. Marion could not believe that after all these years of abuse from Harold she had somehow gotten the courage to stand up to him, and it felt good, real good.

Marion felt her eye sting, and when she looked in the mirror, her eye was swollen, and her face was black and blue from where Harold had slapped her. This was the first time that things had escalated so badly and so quickly. Previously Harold would push Marion, twist her arms, or threaten to slap her, but he never hit her, and even though Marion wanted it all to stop, she never meant to hurt Harold. She reacted from the sting of the blow and the pent-up rage.

As Marion sat in the bathroom, recalling what had just happened, she thought, *I could just have easily swung the poker at Harold's head or some other body part in self-defense and unintentionally killed him. Is it all worth it? Do I need let something tragic happen before I get out of this relationship? I need a reality check, and whether I am ready for it or not, I am going to get it. One day I am going to wake up and realize that I was only holding on to a dream, so I can wake up now or go back to sleep. The situation has never escalated to this.*

Marion again found herself crying out to some unseen person, asking for help. "Somebody, please hear my cry for help and answer me. I am walking down a path of destruction. I need a shoulder to lean on."

Marion's left eye was now swollen shut, and she needed some ice but was scared to leave the bathroom, not knowing if Harold was waiting to attack her again.

Marion waited for a while. When her eye began to hurt more, she went to go to the kitchen to get some ice to put on her face. Harold was, for the first time in all the years Marion could remember, stone faced and quiet, sitting at the dining table with a glass of water. Marion glanced at him to make sure he was not coming at her again, got the ice and a glass of water, and practically ran and bolted herself in her bedroom.

Marion knew that it was late, but she had to call Chloe or Tammy, and after deciding it was best to call Chloe, whom she hoped would be alone, she dialed her number. When Chloe answered, Marion asked Chloe if she was alone, and after Chloe confirmed that she was, Marion recounted what had just happened.

Chloe asked Marion if she was going to be all right in the house with Harold or if she should come and pick her up. Marion told her that this would be a good idea to come and get her so that they both could cool off. Marion told Chloe to come inside to meet her when she got to the house, as she was locked in the bedroom. Chloe said she would be there in about fifteen minutes.

Marion heard when Chloe came, and Harold let her in, and as she heard them talking, Marion took the opportunity to grab her bag with a change of clothes, and bolted for the door, telling Chloe to meet her outside. When Chloe came to the car, she told Marion how sorry Harold said he was and asked if she would forgive him, but Marion told Chloe that she did not want to hear anything Harold had to say, and they left.

CHAPTER 12

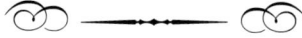

The next morning, not wanting to face Harold, Marion was planning on spending the day in her bedroom when she got home from Chloe's. But when Marion opened the door, Harold was leaning against the wall as if he was waiting for her, and Marion too was ready should Harold try to hit her again, but that was not what Harold was waiting for she soon found out. He was waiting to apologize.

He started to apologize, but Marion hurried past him and again locked herself in the bedroom. Marion did not think of picking up something to eat on the way home and was now getting hungry. She waited to see if Harold would leave the house, but he did not, and Marion was getting hungrier by the minute. Then she heard the front door open and close, and not waiting to see if Harold was actually leaving, Marion ran to the kitchen, intending to make some breakfast and hoard some food for later, as she was not prepared to go to work with a black eye and a face to match. She had no sooner taken the bagel from the refrigerator when she heard the door open and close again.

Marion was caught red handed, as Harold had just gone down the driveway to pick up the morning paper. He was heading for the kitchen, and when he realized that Marion was there, he halted abruptly. He quickly regained his composure and said, "Good morning, Marion."

Marion turned around so that Harold could see her face, intent on asking him if her face looked like it was having a good morning, but before she could say that, Harold saw the ugliness he had created, and he dropped the paper and limped toward her.

"Marion, Marion, I am so sorry. I never meant to hurt you like that."

Marion quickly blocked him off, threatening that if he came any closer she would not be responsible for her actions. Harold tried to reassure Marion that he was not going to do anything to hurt her, and that he was very, very, sorry. Marion told him that she did not want to hear his apology, and she grabbed the food and ran back to her room.

Now Marion was faced with having to call her job to make up an excuse for not coming in to work today and to make up another excuse for Chloe and Tammy, because, even though Chloe came to pick her up last night, Marion still did not tell Chloe everything and still was not sure if she should, and she had yet to face Tammy.

Marion called her job and then started to call Tammy and Chloe, and then she hung up the phone as she thought about what she was going to say. *How could I go on lying to my friends this way? I need to tell them the truth. If they are my friends, they will support me and not judge me. If I can't tell Tammy and Chloe what I am going through, who can I tell? I know Tammy always says she takes all her troubles to God in prayer, but I am not a praying person, so I guess I will have to talk to my friends and let them help me to get some perspective on this situation.*

Marion thought about calling the police to report what had happened last night but did not know if she could have Harold locked up, even after what he did. Then on the other hand Harold had so much rage that maybe that would be a good thing for him. Marion continued pondering whether she should call the police or her friends.

My black and blue eyes and face is all the evidence I need to put him away. Then what? No, I will call Tammy and Chloe. Tammy will know what to do.

Marion again picked up the phone and first dialed Chloe and told her she was going to conference-in Tammy before Chloe could ask her what was going on.

"What's shaking, girl?" Tammy said as she came on the line.

Chloe answered and said, "Certainly not Marion today. She called us so she must be having another crisis and need our intervention."

Tammy ignored Chloe's comment and asked Marion what was going on, and Marion started to cry.

"What! What did I say to upset you? Marion! What's wrong?"

Marion said through her sobs," I just need my two friends right now."

"Say no more," Tammy said. "We are on our way. Where are you, Marion?"

"I am at home," Marion answered through her sobs.

Chloe was the first to arrive at Marion's, and she waited for Tammy to arrive so that they could go in together. Tammy arrived soon after, and they walked up to the door and rang the doorbell. Harold opened the door, and he looked so distraught that Tammy knew something was terribly wrong.

"Is Marion okay?"

Harold just looked down and said, "She is in her bedroom".

Chloe ran ahead to Marion's bedroom, thinking that Harold might have attacked her again, while Tammy walked back to the kitchen with Harold and asked him if he was okay.

Harold broke down in tears and said, "I am so ashamed of myself, and I know that you are going to hate me after today. I am so sorry for hurting Marion."

Tammy became alarmed and said, "Harold, what have you done?"

"I hit her."

Tammy then left him and ran to Marion's bedroom.

When Tammy opened the door and Marion looked up at her, she felt a rage like she had never felt before. The pain and sadness that she saw in Marion's eyes was indescribable.

Marion tried to talk through her tears. "I am so sorry. I am so sorry."

This made Tammy's blood boil, because Marion's face was all black and blue, and she was apologizing.

"What for?" Tammy shouted. "We need to call the police."

"That's what I said," Chloe seconded.

"No, no," Marion said. "Please don't call the police."

"And why not?" Tammy asked.

"I don't want to hurt him anymore, Tammy. I realized that I could have killed him last night," Marion said.

"He could have killed you too, Marion!" Tammy shouted. "How long has Harold been doing this to you? Why couldn't you tell us that the situation was so bad? Don't you trust us, Marion?"

"Yes, I do, but I was too ashamed to let you know that I was going through all this. Your marriage is so perfect, Tammy. How would you understand?"

"Perfect? Marion, you think my marriage is perfect? Well, I have a shocking confession to make, but I will take care of you first," Tammy said.

Tammy just looked at Marion and shook her head and thought, *No wonder so many battered and abused women end up dead.*

Tammy headed the battered women's shelter at her church and never for one moment thought that her best friend was a battered and abused woman. Tammy was so taken aback that she could not find the words to go on. She took a few minutes to calm down then Tammy asked Marion a question that she already knew the answer to, as she had seen it and heard it too often at the shelter. "Do you need us to take you to the hospital or to the police?"

"No, I'll be okay. Harold was hurt more than I was and should probably go to the hospital, and if I go to the police, I could be arrested too."

"Maybe that is what you both need," Tammy said, "in order for you to come to your senses."

At that moment Tammy realized that she had two options. She could report the abuse herself or she could just try to counsel Marion and just maybe she would report it herself or make a decision to leave Harold, but at the moment Tammy also realized that Marion needed the support of her friends. Tammy could see that Chloe was shocked but not as upset as she was, and that raised a red flag within her, so she asked Chloe if she knew this was happening. Marion looked at Chloe, and Chloe looked at Marion, and it was evident that this was not the first time but that it was the first time Tammy knew. She wanted to know why her friends kept this from her.

"Tammy," Marion began, "I am so sorry. I called Chloe last night after Harold and I had the fight. I was too ashamed to let you know. I know that you always said I could do better than accepting second best, and when I see how you live such a wonderful life with Eric, I did not know how to let you know what I was going through, so I turned to Chloe instead.

Tammy did not know what to say and thought about confessing to her friends that things were not always as they seemed and that she too had messed up real bad, but she quickly decided that this was probably not the best time to fess up, so she looked at Chloe, and Chloe looked at Marion, then urged Marion to tell Tammy exactly what she said to her about the situation.

"Don't blame Chloe," Marion said. "You would be proud of her if you knew what she said to me. Chloe told me to get rid of the looser."

"So who is the looser now?" Tammy asked.

Marion hung her head shamefully. "Marion! I am sorry, but I am so upset with you for feeling like you are the victim here. Since you are obviously not prepared to leave Harold, would you mind if I called Eric to talk to him?"

"No, Harold probably could use a friend too, and I think he may need to get his leg and arm looked after."

"What leg? What arm? What happened?" Tammy asked.

"I attacked him with the poker," Marion said, "and he was bleeding last night."

"Oh no, you see, Marion. You need to get out of this relationship before something tragic happens."

"I know, Tammy. I said that very same thing to myself before you came, but I don't have the courage to leave."

"Well, then, let us pray.

Almighty God, you are more willing to hear us than we are to pray. Our pride keeps us from coming humbly before you, and today, oh God, please forgive our ignorance. Please accept this, our humble prayer, as we come into agreement with you for Marion to get the courage and the strength she needs to get out of this terrible situation. Lord, you have called Marion by name. She is your child, and you love and care for her. You want her to experience the abundant life that you have in store for all of us. Show her your will for her life. Grant her the strength and courage she needs at this time, and above all, create in Marion a clean heart, and renew a right spirit within her, and this is my prayer for Jesus Christ's sake, amen."

"Thank you, Tammy! Thank you so very much for praying for me. Do you think Jesus really knows my name and loves me, even though I have been so unlovely?" Marion asked.

"Of course, silly," Tammy told her. "God loves us no matter what, and he is always waiting for us to come to him. His arms are wide open to receive you, so if you are tired, if you are weary, if you are overburdened, he said in the scriptures, "Come unto me all you who are burdened and heavy laden and I will give you rest, for my yoke is easy and my burden is light.'"

"But, Tammy, my thoughts and actions have not been right. I have even been thinking of killing Harold. Will God forgive me?"

"Marion, no matter what we have done or where we have been, God will forgive us, and he could give us a new start, because he is the God of second chances. He is the father of the fatherless, the friend of sinners. He is the omnipotent God. He is able to do for you what no one else could. Just confess your sins before him and ask for his forgiveness, for his guidance and his protection, and he will see you through every problem that you face."

"Tammy, could you teach me how to pray?" Marion asked.

"Marion, praying is easy. It is like talking to your friend. You can tell him anything. You can be honest with him. He will never judge you or get tired of hearing your prayers, and he has already taught us how to pray. In Matthew chapter 6, he told us that he already knows what we need before we ask him but that when we pray, to pray in this manner:

"'Our Father, who art in heaven, Hallowed be your name. Thy kingdom come, thy will be done on earth as it is in heaven. Give us this day our daily bread, and forgive us our debts as we forgive our debtors, and do not lead us into temptation, but deliver us from evil, for thine is the kingdom and the power and the glory, forever and ever, amen.'"

"Oh, Tammy, that was a wonderful prayer. If I forgive Harold, will God forgive me?"

"Of course he will, Marion. He said to us in his word, "For if you forgive men their trespasses, your heavenly Father will also forgive you. But if you do not forgive men their trespasses, neither will your Father forgive your trespasses." His Word does not lie, and all of his promises are true. Just invite him into your heart, and see what he will do for you."

Tammy seemed as stunned as Chloe, who up until this time did not say a word. She had forgotten that Chloe was still in the room until she said, "Tammy, could I invite God into my heart too?"

Tammy was so blown away by what was happening that she just shook her head in agreement.

The three of them knelt down at Marion's bedside, and Tammy began to pray.

"Dear Lord, your Word reminds us that where two and three are gathered in your name, that you are in the midst, and this day, oh God, we are in need of healing, deliverance, forgiveness, and restoration. We are in need of your saving grace. We are in need of your love and your mercy, and I am asking you to accept our prayers, in Jesus's holy name. Amen."

Then, shockingly, Marion started to pray.

"Oh God, I am sinner. I have followed too much the desires of my heart, and they have led me down the wrong paths. Lord, I need you to come into my heart today. I need you to forgive me for all the wrongs that I have done. I need you to make a better a person from this day forward, amen."

Then Chloe prayed. "Lord, I am here with my friends, and I want you to be my friend too, so tell me what I need to do to gain your friendship. How can I draw near to you, Lord? I also want to be a better person, so hear my prayer, oh God, and answer me. Amen."

"Marion!" Tammy shouted. "Where did you learn to pray like that? I never knew that you could pray."

"Tammy, I have listened to you praying a long time, and I just knew that I was in a bad place, and I needed help, and when I opened my mouth, I was shocked too. I still can't believe I just prayed," said Marion.

"And Chloe! I just don't know what to say. Chloe!" Tammy started again, obviously in shock. "Was that for real, or are you mocking me again? This is not the time for your jokes."

"It was real, Tammy. I too have been going through some stuff on my own, and I could not share them with you, but I know that now is not the right time to bring this up, but I too am in need of help. But we can talk about this later."

"No," Tammy said, "If it could bring you to your knees in prayer it must be bad."

And so Chloe began by telling them that she was closing down the business for good, and she started to cry.

Tammy could see Marion was as shocked as she was, and Marion just ran to Chloe and hugged her. Tammy ran to the kitchen to get Chloe a glass of water, and when she returned to the room, Chloe had her shirt pulled up to her neck, revealing some nasty cuts and bruises.

"What in heavens is that?" Tammy screamed.

Marion was just standing there with her mouth wide open, obviously shocked too. Tammy gave Chloe the glass of water and had to hold it up to her lips as she started crying again.

"Tell us what happened, Chloe," Marion finally said.

"I don't know where to begin."

"Well, tell us who hurt you like this."

"It was one of my customers."

"But why? What's his name?" Tammy shouted.

Chloe told them that his name was Danny Loe, and she tried to explain that he was recently dumped by his girlfriend and rented a date for an evening to go to an event where his ex-girlfriend was attending. The next day following the event, he came into the store and angrily accused her of telling his ex that he had rented a date and that he was going to shut down her business.

"I denied his accusations, as this was something I could not have done to any of my clients, and he did not believe me and started harassing me, leaving nasty messages on my phone. I asked him to stop, and he said if I needed him to stop that I should go out on a date with him, and I stupidly agreed. I did not expect a real date with him, and I asked him to meet me at the store after work. When he came to pick me up, I was just closing the store and told him that I would drive my car, and he said it was okay and gave me the address. I told him to give me five minutes and I would finish closing up. I went to the back of the store to turn the lights off, and that is when he grabbed me from behind and tried to rape me."

"Oh no!" Tammy said.

"I tried to fight him off but I was no match for him," Chloe continued. "He raped me and beat me up and said if I ever reported it to the police that he would kill me."

"When was this?" Marion asked.

"It was last Monday," Chloe said.

"Did you see a doctor?" Tammy asked.

"No!" Chloe said. "I was too scared."

"And why didn't you tell me?" Tammy said.

"I was too ashamed to let you see that I had failed yet again. And Tammy, the one thing that kept going through my mind was something that you kept saying to me. 'Chloe, when all else fails, try Jesus.'"

"Chloe," Marion said, "What can we do to help?"

And without giving Chloe a chance to answer, Tammy said, "Right now we need to pray then deal with everything else after," and Tammy began to pray.

"Lord, I just want to thank you for my friends Chloe and Marion. Lord, this is truly a blessing in disguise. You know how long I have been waiting for this day, and look what it took to get us to this place. Lord, your Word did assure us that what was meant to hurt us you will turn it around for our good. My prayer today is that you take us from strength to strength and help us to go forward one step at a time, one day at a time. Amen."

Tammy, Marion, and Chloe then got up and hugged, and Chloe said she felt like a weight was lifted from her shoulders.

Tammy, who then realized that a bond was secured here that would be hard to break, prayed silently, *Lord, where do we go from here? Please show us the way. I am still in need of courage to share with my friends how badly I had fallen.*

Tammy then asked Marion if she should still call Eric to speak with Harold, and Marion said yes, but first there was something that she needed to say to Harold.

Tammy and Chloe followed Marion cautiously to the kitchen where Harold was still sitting, and he jumped up then winced as though in pain. He had a bewildered look on his face as the three of them approached him.

Marion noticed this and assured him that it was all right, that she just had something to say to him.

"Harold," she began, "I forgive you for all the wrong things you have done to me, and I am asking you to forgive me for all the wrong things I have done to you."

"But Marion—"

"No, hold on, Harold. I am not finished. Something happened in my bedroom just now that I still can't believe, but I know it happened, and it feels good. I invited Jesus into my heart. I asked him to make me a better person, and I am hoping that you will do the same. I love you."

Harold was crying uncontrollably. They hugged each other, and he said, "Marion, I would do anything to make it right in your world. Please forgive me. I love you."

Tammy then realized that they both needed this time together, so Tammy told Harold that Eric would come and visit with him, and Tammy and Chloe kissed Marion, and they left.

As they were walking back to the car, Chloe asked Tammy if what happened back there was real. She told Tammy how she was experiencing something that she could not describe.

Tammy then told her that it was the Holy Spirit that now dwells within her and that it was going to take some getting used to, but she would see that it would be all right. Tammy then promised to help Chloe to take baby steps until she was strong enough to run the race for God.

"Chloe," Tammy said, "I want you to know that I will be here for you every step of the way. When you are good and ready, you will come into your own. When you have overcome the shock of what just happened, I want you to meet Pastor Frank, and he will help you also."

They got into their cars and left.

CHAPTER 13

When Tammy got in her car, she called Eric to see if he was at home and told him that she had something incredible to share with him. When Tammy got home, she could hardly hold back the flood gate of emotions that she had fought so hard to keep in check all day after witnessing her two best friends inviting Jesus into their hearts.

Tammy bounded up the stairs to the front door, and as she turned the door knob, Eric was waiting for her, and she just fell into his arms crying.

Eric could see that Tammy was overwhelmed, but he could also see that she was also laughing, and he was just looking at her as though she were crazy.

Tammy just kept saying, "God is good! God is good!"

Eric held her in his arms until she calmed down, then he looked at Tammy and said, "Well, are you going to keep me in suspense all night?"

"Hon, you will never believe what happened today," Tammy said. "Not even after I've told you that Chloe and Marion invited Jesus into their hearts."

"What!" Eric shouted. "What did you do? Oh, no, this was truly an act of God!"

"It sure was," Tammy said, and related what had happened. "I was at my wits end just trying to see how to get those two to go to church with me to no avail, and just like that God moved in a mysterious way, his wonders to perform."

"Well," said Eric, "the journey has just begun, so let us thank God for answered prayers.

"Lord, how good it is when people come to know you, to understand that you are there no matter what, that you will never forsake us when we come to you or ask us why now. You just embrace us with your loving arms. Father, I am so thankful that Chloe and Marion have entered into the fold. Lead them, good shepherd. Lead them beside still waters. Let them be grounded and rooted in your Word. Continue to reveal to them your glory so that they can tell others of your goodness and your mercy and win souls for Christ. All this I ask in your holy name, amen."

"Eric?"

"Yes, Tammy?"

"I need you to please visit with Harold, and I think he needs a friend he can trust. I am really hoping that they could make a brand-new start and live happy, healthy lives."

"I will, Tammy. I will call Eric and see when he would like me to stop by. Today was a great day. I don't even need to tell you about mine, because I surely cannot top this one. I am so proud of you, my love."

"But I don't know what I did," Tammy said. "I just prayed with Marion and told her that Jesus loves her and that no matter what we have done that God will forgive us and that if we are burdened we could give it all over to him, and then Marion asked me to teach her how to pray. Then she prayed. Then Chloe prayed. Yes! Chloe prayed."

"That, my love, was enough. I have been taught and I pass it on in my ministry that all we need to do as Christians is to spread the good news of Christ—his birth, his death, his burial, his resurrection, and his salvation—and to tell the world just what he has done for us and allow others to taste and see for themselves that the Lord is good."

"Fellowship is good, yes," Eric said, "but one could fellowship anywhere, anytime, and the good thing is that God knows just when the time is right for each one of us to come home, and so we just need to encourage all those who are lost and troubled, who are tired, who have failed, who are sick, who are in need, who are burdened and heavy laden to give it over to God, who is the ultimate burden bearer, problem solver, healer, deliverer, and friend."

"So that is how you got your friends who were out there on the streets to join you in fellowship? I always wondered how you got your friends to come to church in the first place. Now they are now upstanding members of the Church of Promise, and you just keep on winning souls for Christ. I am so proud of you, Eric."

"I am proud of you too, Tammy, but this is the reason why I keep telling you to stop harassing your friends to go to church. You see, some Christians believe that going to church is the be-all and the end-all. Fellowship is important, but what is even more important is how you lead others into fellowship. Tammy, I believe that if you claim Jesus Christ as your Lord and Savior and if you are living your life for Christ, then others should see Christ in you."

"Well, honey, I understand that," Tammy replied, "but all my friends are now convinced that it's because of my prayers and my belief in God that I get the things I pray for and why my life seems so full. But to me I am still lacking, because I still can't get some of them to come to church with me, and I am still waiting for God to answer my prayers to have a child."

"Tammy, what you should be doing," Eric said, "is telling your friends just exactly what God has done for you, and maybe they would want to taste and see that the Lord is good. Tell them what God accomplished in you when you trusted him, what he did for you when your back was against the wall and you had nowhere else to turn, no one else to turn to, who rescued you when you sinned and fell short, who gave you a second chance when you were sick and in need and you prayed for God to intercede, how you were healed. These are the things that you need to do to win souls for Christ.

"We read in the book of John chapter 11 when Lazarus had died and Mary and Martha said, 'Lord, if you were here, Lazarus would not have died.' But after Jesus raised Lazarus from the dead, he thanked God, and he told them that Lazarus had to die for God to raise him up so that they would believe. So you too must show others what God has done for you so that they too can believe on the Lord Jesus Christ."

"Well then," Tammy said, "thank you. I have so much to share, because God has done so very much for me. I will especially share my story of how badly I have fallen with Chloe and Marion, because they believe that I am living a perfect life, and I have to show my friends that I am human too and that we all will sin and fall short of the glory of God but that God already knows our frailty and will forgive us when we come to him and repent."

The next morning Tammy called Chloe then conferenced-in Marion to check on them, and they both assured her that they were doing fine. Tammy was so very happy for her two friends. She asked Marion if she was good to go back to work, and she said she would just request a family leave. Harold had to get stitches for his leg, and his arm was broken, so she would need to take care of him. They had talked through most of the night, Marion said, and they agreed that they wanted things to change for the better.

Tammy then told Marion that Eric was going to call on Harold later, and that she needed to speak with both of them about something and wanted them to meet her at her house.

"Is everything okay with you and Eric?" Marion asked. "Oh yes, but there is something that I need to share with you that cannot wait."

"Are you sick?" Chloe asked. "No, well, yes and no, but I will tell you when you get here."

Both Chloe and Marion agreed to meet Tammy at her house.

———— ❖ ————

Eric, meanwhile, had called Harold and arranged to meet with him. When Eric arrived at the house, Harold was in high spirits, despite his injuries. Eric asked him where

Marion was, and he told Eric that Marion wanted to give them some privacy and had gone over to his and Tammy's house. Harold offered Eric a drink, and then he led the way to the living room where they sat down.

CHAPTER 14

"Well, Harold," Eric began, "it seems like the week was very eventful. How's everything?"

"Life in Harold Ville has changed dramatically, and it's not all good, but I am hopeful," Harold replied. "I am so glad that you stopped by, Eric, because you know we as men hate shrinks and the whole idea of counseling, but it's good to be able to talk to a brother who will not be too quick to judge or look down at me but just help me through the bad times. I know that we have not spent a lot of time together recently," Harold continued, "and it's because the marriage was rocky, and I was ashamed to let even my well-meaning friends know that I was failing as a husband. I have been living a lie, Eric, a big fat lie. And you know what the sad part is? I have been lying to myself.

"I thought I had it all—money, the nice home, the expensive cars, prestigious club memberships, a beautiful wife—but I know that I forgot the most important part of the equation. I forgot God. I made time for everything else and everyone else except God. You know how I used to go church and pray? Well over time I guess I got caught up along the way, and I pushed God aside. I forgot to thank the giver of all the good things I have received. I love my wife, but I got too possessive, and I ruined everything because of that. I would give anything to have half the life that you enjoy with Tammy."

"We do have our ups and downs," Eric said to Harold, "but we work everything out through prayer. Harold, I am so glad that you trust me enough for us to be having this long overdue conversation. I always asked Tammy if everything was okay with you and Marion, and I guess I too have failed you as a friend. But to be real honest, the reason why I never really called you to find out how you were doing was because I did not know how to. I did not want to seem like I was prying or pushing you to talk when you were not ready."

"It's not all your fault," Harold said. "I too have been hiding in a sense, because I did not want you or my other friends to know that my controlling ways have turned me into an abusive husband. The good thing is that I understand what got me in this mess in the first place, and I am willing to make the necessary changes to make my marriage a success, but I am going to need your help. I have allowed my pride and my anger to ruin our relationship. I have been so verbally and physically abusive to my wife, and I don't know if I have done irreparable damage to our marriage. I don't know what to do to make things right. Will you help me, Eric, please?"

"You know I will do all I can to help you, Harold," Eric said, "but the first thing we need to do is pray, so allow me to pray for you.

"Dear God, I come into agreement with you for Harold, who has admitted the hurt he has caused his wife in this relationship. He understands that his pride and arrogance, his inability to control his anger and jealousy have led him to do and say things that cannot be undone, but we also know, oh God, that you love us when we come humbly before you, recognizing the wrongs that we have done and asking your forgiveness and guidance. We know that you are a God of second chances. We know that you alone can order our unruly minds. We know that there is no problem, situation, or circumstance greater than you. There is nothing too hard for you.

"Today, oh God, I lift Harold up before you in prayer, and I am asking you to create in him a clean heart and renew a right spirit within him. Lord, he is in need of your guidance. Embrace him with your love. Help him to understand that no matter what he has done or where he has been, that your hand is never too short to help or your ears to heavy to hear his cry for help, and you can give him a brand-new start. Help him to seek you so that he may come to know and to understand that you will be his shelter in times of storms, that he can depend on you to bring him out of all his troubles. He just needs to trust with his whole heart and believe that you are able to do the impossible, and I pray this prayer in the powerful name of Jesus. Amen."

"Thank you for praying such a wonderful prayer for me. I am so glad that you stopped by. You know, Eric, I am really willing to do anything to save my marriage. Before I wanted to save this marriage because I was afraid of what my friends would think or say, but now I really, truly, honestly want a relationship like yours and Tammy's."

"Harold," Eric said, "you don't want a relationship like ours. You want your own, and you and Marion both have to want the same things, work at them together, respect each other, and above all, put God first in all your decision-making, all your needs, and allow him to work your purpose out."

"I remember at one point in my life," Harold said, "when I was always on my knees in prayer, making my requests known to God, but when he answered my prayers, I found less time for him. I became too busy to pray and even busier to go to church, and when I married Marion, I knew that she was not brought up in the church and that we were unevenly yoked from the start, but I still married her to fulfill the desire of my heart, and when she refused to go to church with me, well, I just stopped going. I felt embarrassed that people were asking me every week when Marion was going to come to church with me, and I could not get her to commit."

"Well, Harold," Eric said, "you alone have to decide what is important to you going forward and most importantly, where you want to go from here."

"But where will I begin?" Harold asked.

"I am not a psychologist," Eric said, "but I will tell you man to man that you could begin by telling your wife how sorry you are and work even harder to convince her that you intend to change."

"You think she will believe me?"

"Harold, let your actions outweigh your words. If you tell her that you are sorry and show her how sorry you are, I really believe that time heals all wounds. Well, I see you have your work cut out for you, Harold, so I will leave you to get on with it."

As Eric got up to leave, Harold got up and embraced Eric and said, "I really appreciate your being here for me."

"Anytime, man, anytime," Eric said, and left.

———

Meanwhile, Marion and Chloe had arrived at Tammy's house, anxious to know what was going on. When Tammy let them in the house, they started to bombard her with questions, and she raised her hands to stop them and motioned for them to follow her to the den. Chloe and Marion were now really worried, as this was where they came as a group to dissect and solve problems. Tammy offered coffee to Chloe and Marion, and they refused, saying they wanted to get right down to business, so they sat down.

Tammy began by saying to them that she had let them down badly and that they were going to be shocked to hear what she was going to tell them, but that they must promise not to let the conversation ever leave the den, and both Chloe and Marion agreed.

Tammy said, "Chloe, Marion, we are best friends, right?"

"Yes," they both agreed.

"We don't keep secrets from our friends, right?"

Marion and Chloe hung their heads, knowing they had done just that.

Tammy said, "Okay, let us just agree that going forward we will not keep secrets from each other."

Chloe and Marion then again agreed and urged her to spill it out, whatever it was.

Tammy told them that this was the hardest thing for her to do but something that she must do, especially now, since both of them had not only shared their secret with her, but also accepted Jesus Christ into their hearts.

Tammy said, "As you walk in the Christian way, the road ahead will be bumpy at times, but I want you to know that there will be times when you fall, but it is important that when you do, to just get right back up and keep going."

Marion, as sharp as ever, asked Tammy if she had fallen why she was saying all this.

"No," Chloe said, "people like Tammy, saved and sanctified, Halellujeeer, washed in the blood, as she says, cannot fall. It must be something Eric has done."

When Chloe said this, Tammy started to cry.

"Tammy! Tammy!" shouted Marion and Chloe.

"Are you okay? Do you want us to call Eric?"

"No," Tammy said. "This is so hard for me. I cheated on my husband."

"What!" Marion and Chloe said in unison.

"Not you, Tammy," Chloe said. "Why, how, where, when, with whom?"

"Oh, dear God, no," Marion said. "Is it someone from the church?"

"No," Tammy said, "it was with Max."

"You mean your client Maxwell Thompson, Mr. GQ?" Marion asked.

"Yes," Tammy said.

"Does Eric know?" Chloe asked.

"Yes, he does."

"And you are still together?" Marion asked.

"Yes, we are," Tammy said.

"But how?" Chloe asked. "Did you tell him or… No, no, no! Did he find you and Max together?"

"No," Tammy said, "I told him."

"But why?" Chloe asked. "Are you crazy?"

Marion piped up, "Harold would have killed me."

"I thought about not telling Eric," Tammy said, "but I don't think I would have been able to live with myself."

"Oh no," Chloe said. "You are not as smart as I thought you were. You should not even be telling us this. This is something you take to the grave with you, Tammy."

"No, Chloe, when I married Eric we agreed that we would never keep secrets from each other, and that is why I told him, and I am glad I did, because he has forgiven me, and we are working it out."

Chloe said, "If I knew how to really pray, I would pray for you."

"Could I try to pray for you then, Tammy?" Marion asked.

"Sure," Tammy said. "Practice makes perfect. Just say what is on your mind."

"Dear Lord," Marion began, "we lift up our friend and mentor Tammy before you. You know her heart, oh God, and you know that she is not a bad person, just someone who has made a mistake, a terrible mistake. I am thankful, dear Lord, for her honest heart, for her humility to confess her wrongs before us, knowing that we will not judge her, as she did not judge us, but will support her. Thank you, Lord, for Eric and his ability to forgive Tammy. Lord, help Tammy to never again put her marriage or her service to you at risk by yielding to temptation and falling into sin. Give her and give us also the strength and courage to overcome this, in Jesus's name we pray. Amen."

"That was great, Marion," Tammy said, and both Marion and Chloe came forward and hugged Tammy.

The three of them promised that they would support each as much as possible as they go through these difficult times in their lives.

Tammy said, "I feel like a burden has been lifted from me. Thank you for still loving me despite my mistake."

"Nonsense," Marion said, "you have loved us so many times when we have been unlovely that we could change your name to Saint Lovely Tammy."

Tammy told Marion and Chloe that she had no intention of ever seeing Max again and that she would continue to ask God to strengthen her in the face of any and all sexual temptations. Marion and Chloe and Tammy hugged, and then they turned to leave.

Then Chloe turned around and asked Tammy if she could stay and visit with her a bit longer, and Tammy said yes, so Marion left them alone.

When Marion left, Chloe said to Tammy, "So much has happened today that I am little confused and just needed to speak with you about my fears."

CHAPTER 15

On the way home, Eric could not help thinking about Tammy and just felt grateful for her and the love they shared. He decided then to just stop at the supermarket to pick up Tammy's favorite ice cream to take home for her. Eric was at the checkout stand when he heard someone call his name, and he looked up to see another mentor from the boy's club at church, Larry Walker.

Eric smiled when he saw that he was not alone. Larry was with his wife and their new baby. They had been trying for a long time to have a baby, and that was when Larry started mentoring to fill the void. Eric waited for Larry until he finished checking out, and then they chatted for a few minutes. Larry told Eric that they wanted to christen the baby soon and wanted him to be the godfather. Eric said he would be so delighted. Then they left the store.

The meeting with Larry and the baby brought Eric back to their own struggles of having children. Eric remembered talking to Tammy about the boys in the club whose mother had run off and left them with their aunt and her abusive husband.

I will bring it up to Tammy again to see if she will agree for us to take even one of the boys temporarily. We have explored the possibility of adoption, but Tammy said she wanted to keep trying to get pregnant. I know it's hard for Tammy every time someone else announces in church that they are expecting. But we just keep on praying that one day God will bless us with children of our own.

Eric remembered that Tammy was visiting with Chloe and Marion and called to see if she was home alone.

"Hi, hon," Tammy said. "Where are you?"

"I am on my way home. Are you alone?"

"Yes, I am."

"Did you eat, or do you want me to pick something up for us?"

"No," Tammy said, "I have already taken care of that, so I will see you at home in a bit."

They hung up.

Eric stopped at the mailbox to pick up the mail and was just walking though the door when the house phone rang. He dropped the mail on the kitchen counter and grabbed the phone.

"Hello," Eric said.

"Hi, Eric, it's Marion."

"Hello, Marion, how are you?"

"That is why I am calling. I wanted to thank you for visiting with Harold. I came home just after you left the house, and Harold and I had a chance to really sit down and have a civilized conversation. He said speaking with you made him realize that he needed to make some changes in his life in order to save our marriage, and he was so apologetic for the hurt he had caused me, and I apologized too, as he was not the only one to blame. We agreed to start over again, and I just wanted to say thank you for being there for my husband."

"Not a problem, Marion. Glad I was able to help."

"Eric, I promised Tammy that I would come to church on Sunday, and Harold just told me that he would love to come along with me."

"It would be nice to see you both at church," Eric said. "To God be the glory, great things he has done. See you then. Goodnight."

When Eric hung up the phone, Tammy came into the kitchen and asked, "Who that was on the phone?"

Eric told her it was Marion and told her why she had called.

"That is so wonderful, Eric, really wonderful."

"So did you have a good visit with your girls?" Eric asked.

"Yes," Tammy said, "I had a really good visit with Chloe and Marion."

"So are you going to tell me?" Eric asked.

"Yes, dear," Tammy said. "I will after I have fed my handsome husband."

"I hope you will enjoy dessert," Eric said, "because I picked up your favorite ice cream."

"I know there was a reason I loved you so much," Tammy said.

"Yeah, yeah, food will do it every time," Eric shot back.

Tammy just smiled at Eric and rushed over to kiss him. Tammy then blessed the food, and they sat down to eat. When dinner was over, Tammy dished out two servings of ice cream, and they moved to the den to chat about the day's events.

"Well," Eric said, "how much longer are you going to keep me in suspense? I had a great visit with Harold, but you seem like you were about to burst out of your seams when I came into the kitchen. So what happened?"

"You will not believe this, honey, but I met with Chloe and Marion and told them about my infidelity. It is not something I am proud of, but they look up to me and believe that I am perfect, and after speaking with you today, I realized that I needed to show my friends who I am trying to win over for God, that I am only human and that I too make mistakes, that I too am capable of falling, but that I know how to ask for forgiveness.

"I am so very happy that you have forgiven me, Eric. I know it is going to be a long time before we overcome this, but I promise you that I will never give you any reason to be ashamed of me again."

"I am not ashamed of you, Tammy," Eric said. "I am proud of you, because honestly, I don't know if I could have had the courage to confess to you if this was my falling."

"I believe you would have," Tammy said. "Anyway, Chloe is coming to church with us on Sunday."

"Say what?" Eric exclaimed.

"You heard me. She is really serious about turning over a new leaf, and I could not be happier for her. After Marion left here today, Chloe stayed a while longer and asked me some pretty heavy questions regarding her new commitment to Christ, some of which I told her would be answered as she grew in her walk with God. Chloe was nervous about her new commitment and expressed fears about whether she would be able to walk the walk and not just talk the talk.

"I explained to her that as a new believer, things will seem strange at first until she really comes to grips with the fact that her life is no longer what it used to be, and I told her to just take it one day at a time. I invited her to church and explained to her that she does not have to feel compelled to join my church but that it is important to find a good Bible-based church that teaches about Jesus's birth, death, burial, resurrection, and salvation. I also told her that daily meditation and reflection should be an integral part of every believer's day and that this was encouraged through Bible reading, praying, and fellowship."

"Chloe told me during the visit that she was also worried about what her friends would say about her decision and if she should stop hanging out with them. I told her that I think her friends should be happy for her with whatever decision she makes in her life, that a true friend would encourage and stimulate you to be all that you want to be, and that a true friend would not be quick to judge her or to make fun of her just because the decision she make is not one that they agree with. I also warned her to be prepared, because some of her friends would probably be supportive while others might be critical of her especially her atheist friends."

"I shared with Chloe my own personal experience when I decided to live my life for Christ. I explained to Chloe that I had a lot of friends, some who grew up in

Christian homes and some like herself who did not. And when I gave my life to Christ I struggled for months to understand the changes that were taking place in my life and at the same time found myself in a position where I had to always justify myself to my friends who wanted to know why I could not do this or that with them or go here or there with them. It came to a point where I felt so confused that I started distancing myself from my friends. It was not because I felt that I was now better than they were, but I realized they were adding to my confusion. They were not supportive of my decision to give my life to Christ, and as a result, I had to make a painful decision to cut them off, because they were now traveling a road that seemed so much different than mine, and it was, and I needed to get into a better place in order to deal with them.

"I explained to Chloe that I did not just attend church. I told Chloe that once I became a member, I took an active role in the activities of the church, and I started attending Bible studies, which helped me to grow in my walk with God. I also shared with Chloe that I came to understand from reading the Bible that God gives us talents and resources that he wants us to use for his glory, and that I got involved in and served in various ministries in the church, giving of my time and my talents and resources.

"I also shared with Chloe that I was overwhelmed by the support of other church members who welcomed me with open arms and encouraged me to call on them at any time that I felt the need to talk to someone. It was there that I found a new family at the Church of Promise. I also told Chloe that just as I was embraced as a new member that I would be there for her as others had been there for me, to help her in her walk with God.

"So, you see, Eric, I am looking forward to Sunday very much. Marion told me that she would come also, and I am so happy that Harold will come too."

———•◆•———

Eric was blown away, just listening to his wife. He was so proud of her, and he got up and just took her in his arms and told her how proud he was of her.

Then Tammy asked him how his visit with Harold went. Eric began by telling her how God truly works in mysterious ways, because now, not only were Chloe and Marion coming to church on Sunday, but so was Harold. Eric then told Tammy how Harold said he was willing to do anything to get his marriage back on track and that he wanted to make some changes in his life.

"Well, well," Tammy said, smiling. "Could it get any better than this?"

"It sure could, because I am going to go upstairs and run a nice warm bubble bath for my beautiful wife and then cuddle with her all night long."

"Well then," Tammy said, "it sure could."

CHAPTER 16

When Eric and Tammy arrived at church on Sunday, Chloe was waiting for them. Tammy was so happy to see her that she had to restrain herself from saying that Chloe was finally at church with her. Soon after Marion and Harold arrived, and after exchanging greetings, they went inside

Eric and Tammy stopped from time to time, exchanging greetings and introducing their guests before taking their seats, and from time to time Eric and Tammy looked across at their guests to make sure that they were okay. When the sermon began, to their surprise, the preacher's topic was about forgiveness and second chances. At the conclusion of his sermon, the preacher said he wanted to leave them with a few questions that he hoped they would think about during the week.

"My sermon today was about forgiveness and second chances. There are many of us who at some point in our lives need to forgive someone or have them forgive us, and our hope for this forgiveness is that we all be given a second chance. I will ask you today: Who forgives you of all your sins and is ready and willing to give you a second chance? Will you be ready and willing to forgive someone who has done you wrong or someone you have wronged and hope for a second chance? Let us pray.

"Almighty God, we have all erred and gone astray like lost sheep. We have not loved our neighbors as ourselves. We have done things that only you could forgive, yet, you in your mercy have pardoned us. You will never turn your back on us despite what we have done. You love us, even when we are unlovely. You are always willing to give us a second chance, and so, dear God, teach us to turn the other cheek. Teach us to be likeminded. Teach us to be kind and loving to others, even when they are unlovely.

"Lord, you made us in your image, so teach us your ways. Give us forgiving hearts. Humble us so that we can see the good in every bad situation. We know oh God that you have the power to help and to heal. You have the power to order our unruly minds, and I am asking you, oh God, to visit us at times when we are hurting, when we are confused, when we are in need of your guidance so that we can depend on you to lead us in the right paths, and we pray this prayer in the powerful name of Jesus. Amen.

Following the service, everyone gathered around, shaking hands, catching up on the events for the week, or just wishing someone else a blessed week. It was not something that Chloe nor Harold nor Marion had every experienced, and they said so. Chloe said the sermon was lovely, and the prayer really touched her. She said she never thought about second chances the way the minister explained it. She always wanted a second chance from someone else but found it hard to forgive others.

"Tammy!"

"Yes, Chloe?"

"Can I come back to church with you again? I feel so at home. I feel like I have gained a new family, and I am willing to learn more about your God."

"Chloe," Tammy said, "this God is not just my God but your God too. He made you, and he loves you just the same as he loves me."

"But how can he love me?" Chloe asked. "I am so weak and full of sin."

"Chloe," Tammy said, "if you had a child and that child did something wrong, would you not still love the child?"

"Of course, it would still be my child no matter what, and my love for him or her, that would never change."

"Well, that is the same with you and your Father in heaven. No matter where we have been, what we have done, God still loves us and is waiting for us to come humbly before him and ask for his forgiveness so that he can give us a brand-new start."

"Tammy!"

"Yes, Marion?"

"Would God really give me a second chance too? I have done so many horrible things. I have been so selfish. I have had so many horrible thoughts. Where do I begin? What right do I have to come before God and ask for his forgiveness?"

"Marion, God loves us, and he gives us so many things that we don't ask for because we think we are not deserving of them, but he knows us intimately. He knows our needs before we ask them. He just wants us to come into his presence with thanksgiving, to humble ourselves before him and give him the glory due his name, and all that we ask for he will grant according to his riches in glory in Christ Jesus.

"You ask me where to begin. I will tell you, Marion. God reminds us in Matthew chapter six that we should not be like the Pharisees but to pray in this manner: 'Our Father, who art in heaven, hallowed be thy name, they kingdom come, thy will be done on earth as it is in heaven. Give us this day our daily bread and forgive us our trespasses, as we forgive those who trespass against us, and lead us not into temptation, but deliver us from evil, for thine is the kingdom, the power, and the glory forever and ever. Amen.'"

"Wow!" Chloe and Marion said together.

"Tammy, do you say this prayer every day?"

"As a matter of fact, I do."

"Could I say this every day too, or is it only for people like you who attend church every week?"

"Of course not! Chloe, this prayer is our daily guide. It tells us first that we must honor our Father in heaven. We are reminded of his kingdom in heaven and his promise that his will for us will be completed here on earth. He reminds us that he will give us all that we need for the day. And he reminds us to forgive others who have done us wrong, even as he has forgiven us. He is reminding us that no matter how much we are tempted, his will is not to lead us into temptation, but he is there to deliver us from all evil, and his power and his glory is ours forever."

"Well," Marion said, "I will say this prayer too and hope that I am never tempted to do the things to Harold that I have done in the past. I want to be a better person. Would Harold and I be able to join this church too? What do we have to do?"

"Well," Tammy said, "the first Sunday of every month is newcomers' Sunday. We welcome new people into the church who would like to become members."

"But are they only Christian people like you who are welcomed?" Chloe asked.

"No, silly, we are all sinners saved by God's grace. You know what I am going through right now. If only we could see what is happening in other people's lives, we would not be so hard on ourselves or be ashamed when we fall, because we would see that we are not alone. However, when we dedicate our lives to Christ, we become renewed children of God and are therefore joint heirs with him.

"So," Chloe said, "since we never attended church before today and we have not been praying daily like you do, when Marion and I invited God to come into our hearts at her house, was that not a real dedication to follow Christ?"

"Of course it was. You could invite God into your heart anytime, anywhere. Then you must be baptized into the fellowship of the church. The first thing that needs to happen in the life of an unbeliever who desires to follow Christ is for that individual to acknowledge God and invite him to come into his or her heart and renew a right spirit within him or her, and you both have done that. You will need to confess your sins to God, let him know how truly sorry you are for all that you have done, ask him to show you the way of Salvation and light and to also give you a brand-new start, and he will."

"Tammy," Chloe said, "you make it all sound so easy. What if we decide to do all that you say we should do and we go back to our old ways. "Will God be mad with us? Will he still want to renew a right spirit within us?"

"Oh yes, he will," Tammy said. "No matter how many times you fall along the way, he will be there to pick you up. He will continue to hold your hand. He will carry you when you get too tired to walk, and he will lead you where you should go. All you need to do is to learn to be still in his presence and listen to his voice."

"But how can I hear his voice? Will I be able to hear him as I am hearing you? Do you hear his voice, Tammy?"

"Of course I do, and you will too. He will be that voice that encourages you to follow him, to turn away from doing wrong things. That voice will help you to make the right decisions. All you have to do is to learn to be still in his presence, and you will hear his voice loud and clear, but know that this will not happen overnight."

"You know, Tammy," Marion said, "I believe I have heard God's voice before, but I did not know him and still don't know what it means to be still in God's presence, but I believe that I have heard his voice before."

"One day," she said, "I was having this fight with Harold, and it had gotten so ugly that I picked up a dumbbell to throw at him, and when I turned around, I felt this sharp pain in my arm that prevented me from throwing it at him, and something in my head, I still believe it was something in my head, said, 'Marion, what if you hit him and he falls dead at your feet? What will happen to you? You will go to jail, and will it be worth it?'

"I immediately dropped the dumbbell. and when I looked up at Harold, all of the anger I felt just vanished, and I thought it was because of the pain in my arm, but after hearing what you just said to me about hearing God's voice, when I think back on that incident I now believe that it was God who saved me from what could have turned out terribly."

"So that is how God speaks to us, through our consciences?" Chloe asked

"Absolutely," Tammy said. "God has given us a spirit of discernment to know right from wrong, and being a Christian means that you must always be obedient to God, and that is why we read the Bible to understand what he requires of us, the kind of lives we should live as Christians. There are two main things that he asks of us: to love him and serve him with all of heart and soul and mind and strength, and to love our neighbors as ourselves."

"Hold up. Wait a minute," Chloe said. "You mean I must love my peeping Tom neighbor Rodney as myself, that I must treat others the same way I treat myself? What if I don't like the person? Only you would do something so stupid, Tammy."

"It's not stupid, Chloe, but you will understand one day if you continue to allow God to be the Lord and master of your life. You will begin to look at others differently. You will want to help people who are less fortunate. You will be forgiving, especially to those who have hurt you, those who have done you wrong. You will be happy to spend quality time with God. You will be a totally new person, and the Bible tells us that when we accept the Lord as our personal savior, we are born again. We are a new creation. Old things are passed away, and we are made brand new from the inside out.

"Others will see the difference in you. They will want to know the secret of your success and the source of your joy, and then you will be able to tell them that the God you serve is a God of second chances. You will be telling others what he has done for you, and that if he changed you into the creature that you are, he could change them too. All they need is a reason to believe that God is all powerful and that he is a God who is able to do the impossible."

"Chloe," Marion said, "Tammy has convinced me that there is a better way, God's way. Are you convinced?"

"I am, Marion. Tammy, will you please help us?"

"Yes, I will. You could also come back to church with us again next Sunday, and if you still feel this way, I could ask the minister to speak with you about getting baptized."

"We would love to get baptized, but, Tammy, could you explain to us why we have to get baptized?" Chloe asked.

"When one is received into the household of faith," Tammy said, "it is through baptism that one is truly committed to walking in God's way, to be his disciples. We read in Matthew twenty-eight, nineteen through twenty: 'Therefore, go and make disciples of all nations, baptizing them in the name of the Father, and of the

Son and of the Holy Spirit and teaching them to obey everything I have commanded you.'"

"Wow," Chloe said, "maybe we should invite God into our hearts again here in church today. It will make it seem more real."

"Could we, Tammy?" Marion asked.

"Yes, you could."

"You mean right here?" Chloe asked.

"Yes, just say this after me.

Dear God, I come before you this day, asking you to come into my heart. I want to accept you as the Lord and master of my life. I want you to create in me a clean heart and to renew a right spirit within me. Lord, I am not perfect. I have walked in my own sinful way. I have followed too much the desires of my own heart. I have been weak and sinful, and I have not loved you with my whole heart.

"I have not loved my neighbor as myself. I did not know how to give you thanks and praise for all the many times you have protected me from harm and danger, for providing for my needs, but I recognize now that you are all powerful and that you understand my frailty. You are my Father who loves me and wants the best for me.

"So dear God, I am choosing to serve you from this day forward. I will study your Word so that it will become a light unto my feet and a lamp unto my path. I will trust you to pick me up when I fall and to sustain me through troubled times. Lord, I now believe that there is always another way, a better way—your way. And I will trust you with all of my heart and mind and strength. In Jesus's holy name I pray. Amen."

As they stood there embracing, Harold and Eric walked up to them. Harold had a smile on his face that shone like the sun and so did Eric.

"What's going on with you two?" Chloe asked.

"Marion," Harold said, "you will not believe what just happened."

"What, Harold?"

"I am still so shaken up by what just happened that I will let Eric explain."

"Well," Eric said, "God moves in a mysterious ways, his wonders to perform. He plants his footsteps in the sea and rides upon the storm! Would you know that Harold just accepted the Lord as his personal Savior and agreed to become a member of the Church of Promise?"

"What!" Marion said and rushed to hug her husband. "Praise the Lord!"

"Ladies, I think you all have something to share also," Tammy said.

"Well," Chloe began, "we also accepted the Lord as the Lord and master of our lives and are thinking of getting baptized and become members of the Church of Promise."

"How did that happen?" Eric asked.

"Well," said Tammy, "God did it, and I think this should be a celebration moment. Why don't we all go out to lunch and celebrate the goodness of the Lord in a mighty way?"

The others agreed, and the five of them went to lunch.

They had such a great time that they all agreed to make this a weekly event where they could catch up with each other.

On the way home from lunch, Tammy and Eric were so happy for their friends that they stopped at the bookstore and got them each a Bible. They then went home and spent the rest of the afternoon together.

CHAPTER 17

Then next day after work, Eric went to the church to mentor as usual at the Little Wanders Club. When he got there, instead of all the boys playing outside, only a few cars were parked, and there was no sign of the boys.

When he went inside, the pastor said to him, "Eric, we are glad you could make it today."

"What's going on, Pastor? I did not say I was not going to be here today."

"No, but we are glad that you are here, because we have some good news for you. Come with me."

Eric followed him into his office.

A lady Eric did not recognize and another gentleman were already seated in the office. The pastor introduced them to him as Mr. and Mrs. Rancher, whom he explained were long-time friends of his and who ran an orphanage in Miami. He further explained that they were visiting with him, and in their conversation they mentioned that a six-week-old baby girl was dropped off at the orphanage just last week and that they were trying to find a home for the baby.

I then told them that I knew the perfect couple that would welcome this new baby with open arms, and that was why they were here to talk to you Eric.

"If you and Tammy are still interested, that is, I will leave it up to you to discuss this."

Eric was so shocked he was unable to speak for a few minutes. He knew that Tammy would be overjoyed, as they were trying for years to have a baby without any success, and now here they were being given the opportunity to be parents.

"Thank you," he said when he found his voice again. "Could I please call my wife and let her know this?"

"Of course," said Mr. and Mrs. Rancher.

Eric then excused himself from the room and called Tammy, who was just getting home from work.

"Tammy!"

"Yes, Eric?"

"Are you sitting down?"

"No, I am not," she said.

"Well, you had better sit down, because I have something to tell you that will take your breath away."

"Okay. What?"

"Well, how do you feel about adopting a six-week-old baby girl?"

"Wow! What? Wait! What did you say? We are being offered a six-week-old baby girl to adopt? When? Where? Who?"

"Take it easy. I will get all of the information for you, and then we can go from there."

"Oh, glory be to God," Tammy said. "Thank you, God, for answering our prayers. We give you the honor and the glory due your name, and we will continue to give you all the praise, because you are wonderful. Praise the Lord."

Eric then went back into the office and told the Ranchers that his wife was overjoyed. They made arrangements to meet again and for them to see the baby and begin the adoption process.

Meanwhile, Tammy was on the phone three-way calling her mother, Marion, and Chloe, telling them the good news. When Eric got home, he filled her in on the rest of the conversation, and they enjoyed a quiet celebration at home.

Over the course of the next two months, while they awaited the adoption to be final, Tammy was busy getting the nursery ready to bring home the baby. There was so much to do, and Tammy wasted no time. With the help of her two friends, the nursery was ready in no time. Everything went smoother than they had imagined. They passed their background checks with flying colors, their visits with the baby were going well, and they were just waiting for everything to be finalized to bring the baby home. Tammy was overjoyed and so thankful to God for bringing this baby into their lives.

"Dear God," she prayed, "I will bring this child up in the right way with your help. We are depending on you to continually watch over her and protect her. Lord, we have waited so long for this baby, but we know that this is the right time, because you are an on-time God, and I just want to give you the honor and the glory due your name. Lord, I am thankful that I know how to wait on you for the good things you have in store for me and most importantly how to wait patiently on you."

On the day the baby was due to arrive home, Marion and Chloe hung banners outside saying, "Welcome home, Terica," the name Tammy and Eric had chosen for the baby. Pink and white balloons hung everywhere.

When Tammy and Eric pulled up outside, they all rushed to the door with welcoming smiles. The pastor was on hand to pray for the new baby and for Eric and Tammy, who were parents at last.

They stayed a while with them, but baby Terica was getting a little flustered. She was overwhelmed by all the attention and the new surroundings, so they decided to give the new parents some bonding time and left.

CHAPTER 18

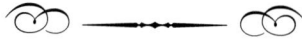

Harold and Marion went home, and Chloe left to catch up with Ben, her new friend from church. Chloe met Ben during the newcomers' reception, and they were inseparable ever since. Ben was Senior Warden for the church, and even though Chloe claimed that they were just friends, everyone could see that this friendship was blossoming right before their eyes.

Chloe could not believe that she had found the man of her dreams in church when all along she was in the clubs and on dating sites trying to hook up with Mister Right. Ben was paying her all the right compliments, treating her like a lady should be treated, and was slowly but surely winning her over.

"I thought Christians were boring people," Chloe said, "but I was wrong."

Marion was leading the entertainment committee, and boy, did she know how to organize some fun events. They went bowling, had game nights, had pot luck dinners, had Bazaars, and had trips to various destinations. They just did not know what Marion would come up with next, and Ben was Chloe's date, chaperone, and escort to every single event.

Chloe was now well settled into Church of Promise, as were Harold and Marion. Chloe was finally in love.

Just last week, Chloe had secretly told Marion and Tammy that they did not want to wait much longer to get married. When they asked her what was the rush and if she was pregnant, Chloe said no, but the temptations were becoming too great, and according to Scripture, if they couldn't abstain, they needed to get married, so they were planning to get married next month and wanted to know if they would help her to arrange it.

Chloe said they were not planning on a big wedding, and Marion and Tammy agreed to help. After the wedding date was set for June third, everything swung into high gear. There was the shower to plan and arrangements to be made. Everything had to be perfect for Chloe's wedding, and both Tammy and Marion wasted no time in getting everything ready to perfection.

The day of the wedding dawned bright and clear. It was a beautiful day, and everything went according to plan. Chloe was so radiant, and Ben was so handsome. Harold and Marion sang a beautiful rendition of "Blest Be the Ties that Bind Our Hearts in Christian Love."

Chloe was blown away, because never had she imagined being married to anyone like Ben, an upstanding member of the church, and to hear this rendition by her friends that summed it all up, the binding of their hearts in Christian love.

Immediately following the ceremony and the reception, they were both whisked off to their honeymoon arranged by Harold and Eric to the beautiful Caribbean Island of the Montserrat for two glorious weeks.

CHAPTER 19

Meanwhile, life for Harold and Marion was getting better. Giving their lives over to God did not only transform them, but renewed their marriage as well. They were both regularly attending counseling, despite Harold's opposition to it. But he recognized that he needed to do whatever it took to get his marriage back on track. Harold was a mentor at Little Wanderers and was on the choir. Marion was involved in several of the church missions, and she was teaching Sunday school and finally trying to get pregnant.

Harold was sweeter than Splenda on a honey bun to Marion, who could not soak it up fast enough. They were no longer just tolerating each other but really enjoying each other's company. Marion was again the proud hostess of Harold's events, and now her favorite line was, "Oh, what a little prayer can do!" She was now an advocate of, "Is there any time left for God?"

She recalled the many times when Tammy would ask her to go to church with her or to go to the soup kitchen to help or to visit the homes or hospitals with her, and she would find a reason to say no, which always left Tammy asking the question, " Is there any time left for God?" Now she had repeated that line more times that she could count.

Marion was now constantly sharing her story with others, telling them that when her house was full she had no time for God or anyone else but that when the full house no longer brought her comfort that God showed her a better way—his way. Marion was constantly reminding others that they should never be too prideful or boastful about what they had attained, because all that they had, all that they would be they owed to the glory of God. Marion said she now understood that God allowed her to operate in her own sinful way but that he had a plan all along to show her in his own time who was in control.

Marion decided that she would initiate a mission at Church of Promise called, "Is there any time left for God?" This mission would encourage people who had lost their faith, people who were struggling in the faith, people who did not know Christ in an intimate way, and people who just needed a reason to believe, to have the resources that they needed to grow in their faith or come to know God in an intimate way—just as she and Harold had done.

Marion and Harold now began and ended every day with prayer. They spent quality time with God in prayer. They knew how to bring their petitions before God, and most importantly to be still in his presence and wait patiently for him to act.

Marion said when she was walking in darkness that she did not know how to pray, that when her eyes were closed to the goodness of the Lord she did not know how to trust God for anything. But now she was so very thankful that her family was saved and that because they now made time for God, he kept opening more doors for them to walk through every day. They now had a balanced life, where Harold could hang out with his friends and Marion could do the same without having to question each other.

CHAPTER 20

Marion later called Tammy and Chloe, and they agreed to meet at Sawgrass Mall. When they arrived at the mall, Tammy surprised them by announcing that not only did she have to shop for Terica, who was growing out of her clothes so fast, but that they were going to be aunties again, as she just found out that she was pregnant with twin boys.

"Well," Marion said, "God surely rewards double for trouble, and there is no time to waste. I have to now not only make time for God but squeeze all of you into my day. But I now know that when I make time for God, it becomes easier for me to fit everyone and everything else into my day. Let us pray.

"Dear Lord, we have so much to be thankful for today. You have given us so much. Where do we begin to thank you? I just want to thank you for bringing Tammy into my life to help to show me the way to you. Tammy has been so patient with me, with us. She has been such a true friend to us. How could we ever repay her?

"Lord, we know that you bring people into our lives for a reason and a season. Tammy still has so much to share with us, so we ask that you continue to use her to be a blessing to us so that we in turn can be a blessing to each other. Lord, we are thanking you today for answered prayers, for pouring out a double blessing on Tammy, and we ask that you watch over her as she goes through this pregnancy. Lord, I am thankful for Chloe, who is determined to soldier on for you. May her walk with you be strengthened daily, in Jesus's name we pray. Amen."

"Well, thank you, Marion, for that wonderful prayer," Tammy said. "I know just how you could repay me. You have given me so much joy just to hear you give thanks and praise to God. I remember not long ago when you asked me to teach you how to pray. Now you could repay me by being the same kind of friend to someone else that I have been to you and help to lead someone else to Christ.

"Always remember that you cannot live your life for your friends, but allow them see God's life-light shining through you. A true friend should not be quick to judge you or rejoice in your tribulation. A true friend stands by you through thick or thin. A true friend lets you know when you are doing something wrong. A true friend is there to pick you up when you fall, to encourage you when you are weak. So, my friend, continue on in God's strength. Be a soldier for Christ every day. Encourage one another. Never let your day become so full that you don't have any time left for God."

"When you see others around you who don't have any time in their busy schedules for God, you just ask them the same question I asked you and kept asking you: Is there any time left for God? I am sure that you are going to get the same answer you gave me not so long ago, but you will have a story to share, your own story of how not long ago you thought God was the one who had time and did not need yours. And you will tell them what happened when your back was against the wall, when you felt like all hope was lost, how God delivered you and now, how you make time for God, to spend quality time in his presence, and how he continues to turn things around for you. You just tell them about your awesome God and what he has done for you, and just walk away singing, 'Oh, how good it is to know I know the Lord.'

"Marion and Chloe," Tammy said, "God has been carrying you, carrying us, through the storms of life, and every day it will get sweeter, the intimate relationship we have with God. I could tell you this, my friends that I have run the race for God, and I am still running. I have fought the good fight, and I am still fighting, but I know that when the fight goes out of me, God will be my armor bearer. When I have struggled and I am overburdened, God will take my yoke upon him. All that I have been through and because of my faith in God, I now handle things in a different way, and I know how to take everything to God in prayer."

"Well," Chloe said, "this is all good, but Terica will not stay the same size forever, and the twins can't run around naked, so we have some shopping to do."

They later closed down the mall, and armed with their shopping bags, they followed Tammy to her car and helped her pack the stuff in. Then they hugged, and they reminded each other of the weekly lunch on Sunday to catch up.

CHAPTER 21

The Sunday after-church lunch date was now the norm for Tammy, Eric, Marion, Harold, Chloe, and Ben. So every week they would have lunch and just enjoy each other's company. Christmas was fast approaching, and they all got so caught up in their own affairs that finding time to get together was almost impossible. So they decided that they would all celebrate the holiday at one house, and it was decided that they were going to Chloe and Ben's, since this would be their first Christmas as husband and wife.

Following the conclusion of the Christmas day service, they all went out to Chloe and Ben's house, and it was just like old times. Harold and Marion were not at each other's throats, Terica was growing up so fast, and Tammy's twins were due any day now. Eric was a sweet as ever. They were having a really good time.

After they were finished opening up their presents, Chloe told them that there was one gift left to be opened.

"Well," she began, "this is the gift that keeps on giving, and this is just the right time and place to announce to our friends that we are expecting our first baby!"

Cheers went up all around them. They were all so happy for the newlyweds. Chloe told them that Ben was overjoyed when she told him that she thought she was pregnant and he urged her to immediately go and see the doctor, who confirmed that she was indeed six weeks pregnant.

"Wow," said Eric, "you wasted no time, Ben."

"It was not me," Ben said. "It was God smiling down at us, and we wanted our friends to be the first to know."

Chloe nudged Ben, who had apple cider chilling in the refrigerator to celebrate the occasion, and he tapped on his glass to signal attention while at the same time announcing that he would like to make a toast to Chloe, his beautiful wife and soon-to-be mother of his child.

"Well, Chloe," Marion said, "it looks like we both will be pushing strollers at the same time!"

"What?" Harold jumped out of his chair and swung a fist in the air, saying, "Yes!" Then he swooped up his wife and kissed her, asking her if she was really pregnant and why she did not say anything.

"We had so many false alarms and miscarriages," she said, "that I wanted to be sure, and I just got the results yesterday and wanted to wait a few weeks before making any announcement. I did not mean to rain on Chloe's parade, but I couldn't stop myself."

So after Ben had poured more apple cider in their glasses, a proud and beaming Harold got up, helped Marion to her feet, and placed his arm on her stomach. "Finally, I am going to be a dad. Marion, I will treat you like a princess from this day forward. I cannot thank you enough for giving me this gift."

Marion was speechless. She was so happy to hear Harold say these wonderful things in front of their friends.

Tammy just wrapped her arms around her and said, "Eric and I are both so happy for you and are officially putting you on notice that we are going to be the godparents."

"So what about me?" Chloe asked.

"You know without a doubt Chloe that you will be Aunty Chloe."

Ben was grinning from ear to ear. They could see how much he adored Chloe and how much this child would mean to them.

Eric could recount the many times Ben had to console him after Tammy's miscarriages. Eric gave everyone else a chance to congratulate them then he got up and gave Ben a man hug and said, "Yes! That's what I am talking about! Who's the man? Who's the man!"

And they both gave one another high fives and bumped shoulders together while their wives just looked on, having a good laugh.

"Well," Harold said, "where's the love?"

Eric said, "I did not forget you. Come here, ole man. Gimme some skin. This occasion really calls for another round of apple cider, and this one is on me."

"So," said Tammy, "do you want a boy or a girl?"

"We don't really care," Marion answered. "We just want to have a healthy baby. Will you please keep me in your prayers as I go through my pregnancy?"

"We sure will," they all said.

CHAPTER 22

Tammy then said, "Let us pray.

Dear God, you are truly the giver of all good gifts. We are so very thankful for these blessings, and most importantly we are thankful that you sent your Son, Jesus, the Savior of the world. It is because of him we are able to celebrate this glorious Christmas season, and may we never forget that you are the reason for the season and the giver of all the many good gifts we receive. We will always keep Christ in Christmas and in our homes."

Harold then decided that he wanted to lead them in prayer, saying how especially grateful he was to God for restoring and renewing and extending his family.

Then Marion bowed her head and began to pray.

"Heavenly Father, let your peace dwell in our hearts today. Send us your Holy Spirit to lead and guide us in the right way. May we never become too busy that we push you aside. May we always remember where you brought us from. Help us to understand that in you is a sweet peace and that walking with you side by side, feeling your presence, your gentle touch is all we need.

"Lord, your peace and your calming spirit within us can see us through the problems of this life. We just need to put you first in all things. We will give you our first waking moments, and all through the day we will lift you up in praise. And at evening time we will give you the honor and glory due your name. We will make this a habit so that we will never have to wonder if there is any time left for you, but to make time for you. Amen."

"Well, then, I guess it's my turn to pray," Ben said.

"Heavenly Father, you alone know the desires of our hearts, and you give us our fruits in due season. My hands have been lifted up before you for so many years asking for a wife and children, and you truly give us those things that we ask, but in your own time. I am especially thankful for this new family that you have given me, and from this day forward as for me and my house, we will serve you. We will never forget that you are the source of all the good things that we receive. Lord, I am thankful for my extended family—Harold, Marion, Eric, and Tammy. Continually bind us together in love for Christ's sake. Amen."

Eric then got up and said, "Well, it's time for the Christmas carols. Who is going to lead us?"

Marion said, "Harold will, of course. You all have come to appreciate him singing in the choir. I can't wait for him to begin singing to the little one."

Harold said that he could not think of a better carol to begin with than "Away in a Manger." They sang every Christmas carol they could recite from memory then finished with, "We Wish You a Merry Christmas," vowing to always keep Christ in Christmas.

Eric then said he wanted to have some man time with his friends, and Tammy, Chloe, and Marion were happy to see them go.

They wanted to hear all about how Chloe got so lucky when they had all waited for such a long time to get pregnant.

The guys, meanwhile, went out to Sporty's Grill to celebrate.

When they were ready to leave, Eric called for the check, but Harold said, "No, I got you."

And Ben said, "No, we got you."

Eric said, "No, I got both of you. This is my treat. Congratulations, big fellas!"

Is There Any Time Left for God, by Jewellyn
Greer is available wherever books are sold
as both a printed book or an e-book.

For more information about the book
including information about speaking
engagements, please email the author at:

jewellyngreerministries@yahoo.com

Follow us daily on Facebook for daily
inspirational posts and updates:

http://www.facebook.com/PrayersforEverydayLiving